MANFRED GÖRK

LOCKDOWN IN NEW ZEALAND

AF284106

About the Author and this Book

Manfred Görk, born in 1954, studied economics and now lives in Heidelberg, Germany. His professional activities led him around the globe. He got to know countries, cultures and people who shaped him. After his professional career, he turned to writing. He is an outspoken connoisseur of China and made life in that country the essential content of his books and video films. For current reasons, the so-called Corona-Crisis and its fight in New Zealand, he presents this diary today.

Other publications:
Land der Mitte - Impressionen aus einer anderen Welt (2017, ISBN: 978-3-9584057-0-7). This book has also been published in Chinese translation (2018, ISBN: 978-3-7481990-9-0).
Luluba – Geschichte einer chinesischen Bauernfamilie (2019, ISBN: 978-3-749-44872-2).

Contact: landdermitte@gmx.net.

Manfred Görk

Lockdown in New Zealand

CORONA Travel-Diary

Translation of the original German edition

Bibliographic information of the German National Library:
The German National Library records this publication in the German
National Bibliography; detailed bibliographic data is available on the In-
ternet http://dnb.dnb.de.

Cover design: Manfred Görk

Source of cover element: <a href='https://pngtree.com/so/behand-
lung'>behandlung png from pngtree.com</a>

Production and publishing: BoD – Books on Demand, Norderstedt

ISBN: 978-3-751-93512-8

To those who

break the chain of transmission

STAY HOME

BE KIND

(Jacinda Ardern)

Table of Contents

Foreword

In January 2020, the world began to change in a way that no one had experienced before, with the exception of those who had experienced the Second World War. A virus attacked people, first in China. While the number of people infected there is rising dramatically every day, the West felt safe and made no arrangements to prevent, or at least make it more difficult, to spread to its own population. At the end of February, it became clear that the Western world was not immune to the virus, but people were still living unimpressed. They lived according to their regular plans, fueled by governments that still spoke of a local East Asian affair.

Sven Neuland and Wei Ling had set off on a big trip to New Zealand. When they arrived, the virus was far away. Then, after three carefree weeks, their journey came to a sudden halt. In New Zealand, the highest Alert Level, the national emergency, has been declared and all public life has been brought to a standstill. The virus had also reached the remote island nation. There was only one goal for the government: to eliminate the virus. Sven and Ling, like tens of thousands of other tourists, language students, globetrotters, had to go into self-isolation without knowing how long this state would last. In this situation, most foreigners felt that the quick return to their home country was the most sensible destination, but many hurdles stood in the way of implementation.

Mr. Neuland and Mrs. Wei told me the very personal story and perception of their isolation, their lockdown in New Zealand. They gave me permission to publish their records. The diary begins with the description of their first very normal vacation days. But from the very beginning on, the Corona virus, which had become known as COVID-19, was already pushing into everyday life. The period of perseverance during the nationwide lockdown was marked by daily, even hourly, dealing with the virus. It determined the days and nights while waiting for the return flight. The thinking and feeling during this time were directly and strongly influenced by COVID-19. From their story, one learns what the virus did to humans, apart from a possible physical infection. I would like to make this diary available to the interested public as early as possible because of the topicality of the subject. Therefore, translation, orthographic and grammatical errors may have crept into the text. I apologize.

May 2020, Manfred Görk

Preparation

Actually, Ling and Sven had a very different plan. The hope of realizing it, possibly with a few variations, is stomped within a few days. This was the fault of the Middle Kingdom, Sven read in the Western media. Guilt was a virus, was fear. On January 26, his wife Wei Ling flew back to China, where there were a few things to do for her. What she had to do in Germany was completed. Ling's flight via Shanghai to Auckland was scheduled for February 17. Sven Neuland would meet her there a day later to explore the other end of the world together with her. Afterwards they wanted to fly to China together and return to Germany in mid-April. That was the plan. Sven had bought the plane tickets, booked rental cars and a number of motels, and worked out a rough itinerary. On the eve of January 26, Ling's first concerns arose. Was it not too risky to go there now because of the large number of people already infected with the virus in their home country? After all, more than 2,000 Chinese have already been infected, although no one in her province. Wouldn't it be safer to stay in Germany, a country whose government was convinced that this evil virus did not pose a threat to its people?

A few days earlier, Mrs. Wei had taken the final step in obtaining the residence permit, the successful language examination with flying colors. Seven weeks of hard, independent learning were crowned by success. She had submitted all the documents for the acquisition of the residence permit to the Citizen's Office, at the same time had registered her residence in Germany, everything went according to plan. She could have stayed. Sven Neuland also felt doubts about the correctness of the decision, but he encouraged his wife to fly anyway. She would only be in China for a few days, barely three weeks in total, since not much unexpected could occur. At the time, they had no idea how endlessly long three weeks would be in the days of COVID-19.

Mrs. Wei flew. A strict curfew had also been imposed in her province, but she was still allowed to travel to her home and go to her own apartment. Apart from a large food purchase once a week, no other activities outside the apartment were allowed. She couldn't do any of the planned activities, neither meet friends nor family in person. It was quickly clear that this condition would not change for quite some time. Every day in the apartment was a boring wait for the next monotonous day. Every day, the number of people infected increased significantly. The virus spread in waves across all Chinese provinces.

Germany was safe, the whole West was not in danger, even non-communist Asia was without any hazard. This is what the media reported on a daily basis. Above all, New Zealand was safe, both knew that. To ensure that this remained the case, the island nation at the other end of the world had already imposed a ban on Chinese entry. It concerned those who had been in China in the last 14 days before entering China. Other countries, such as Singapore, made the same decisions. Ling's flight from Shanghai to Auckland was therefore cancelled. The devil, hidden in the virus, still seemed local, but the plan of their trip to New Zealand was shattered like a soap bubble.

Mr. Neuland was no one to give up quickly. He played through various scenarios, while focusing on his wife's safety, but still stuck to the plan of the New Zealand trip, albeit at a different time.

Mrs. Wei had been in her home isolation for ten days. The number of people infected with the virus continued to increase daily. So far, cases in her province have been low, but it was clear to everyone that the Chinese government would take further restrictive measures within hours at the slightest sign of aggravation. There were still flights to Germany, but their number had already been greatly reduced and the vacancies had shrunk to a single-digit number. They decided on February 6 that Mrs. Wei should fly back to Germany as soon as possible. Ling reached for her mobile phone, dialed Air China's phone number to end up in a queue. This was completely new for Chinese. It was clear that others had the same plan, it was in a hurry. Chinese were not prissy when they wanted a service. Mrs. Wei called the VIP hotline, even though she wasn't even nearly a VIP of the airline. But before the employee could alert her to it, she had already given to him her booking request. It was easier for the nice gentleman on the phone to book the flight for her.

Two days later, she was already on the plane. On the way via Beijing to Frankfurt, she was checked three times. Fever was measured by people wearing protective suits and fully covered face. The paths in the airport terminals were closed in a way that the usual strolling through the shops was no longer possible. Health questionnaires had to be completed and wearing a mask was mandatory, both at the airport and during the flight. For Chinese, this was nothing unusual, they would have done it themselves without an order.

In Frankfurt, she got off the plane the next morning and immediately felt that she had arrived in a free country. Germany was obviously immune to such a Chinese virus. No one was checked at the airport; no health questionnaires were issued and fever was not measured. So, like everyone else, she walked out of the arrivals hall as if there was no COVID-19. Meanwhile, Lufthansa and many other airlines had suspended their flights to China, but Chinese airlines were still allowed to fly and spit out well over 1,000 people every day in the country that did not consider it necessary to carry out even a minimum of controls.

The virus piped up for the first time: You Germans will still bitterly regret it. Very soon! It still went unheard.

Everyone greeted Mrs. Wei when she was back in Germany. She had made the only right decision, she was told. And that proved to be the case immediately, because a lot of things were now smooth. If the virus had believed that it could re-enter the thoughts of Mr. Neuland and Mrs. Wei, then it was mistaken.

Mrs. Wei was granted a residence permit on February 20. However, the issue of the corresponding card with the name eAT (electronic residence authorization title) will probably take four weeks, she learned from the Immigration Office. What's the point, Wei Ling could still use her visa until July anyway.

With a heavy heart, Mr. Neuland began to cancel all bookings of motels, flights and rental cars. He had planned well. With the exception of a ridiculous 50 Euros, everything went at no extra charge. While he was canceling, he formed a new plan. It was almost the mirror image of the first, starting only two weeks later. This deadline had to be met also because of the transit rules for the ports of call. Because they had to fly later and the autumn would arrive in New Zealand, he simply reversed the order. At first, they would stay on the South Island, and then, with the warmth, let themselves drift further and further north. A wise decision. At that time, however, he did not know that it was a brilliant move for other reasons as well.

Their departure was now scheduled for March 2. In the final days before the departure date, Mr. Neuland called Singapore and New Zealand almost daily to ensure that the «14-day non-China stay» rule remained in place. It was confirmed to him. He had planned the return flight with Qatar Airways. It was a good time to make a three-day stopover in Doha. That, too, he had booked. Singapore Airlines would bring the two to New Zealand, Qatar Airways would bring them back. Then the eAT, would also be ready for collection in the Citizen's

Office. Despite the complicated Corona situation in China, a good plan. They were extremely satisfied with it and full of anticipation.

A good friend: Is it a wise decision to fly now?

This was a question that you knew when you were asking it that it couldn't be answered easily.

The virus interfered in the search for an answer: I not only infect the lungs; I also confuse the mind of the people.

Sven: We have everything under control, we are well prepared. He recalled the central statements of his country's government. The figures proved it was right, as it believed, or at least wanted to tell the population. A day before departure, Germany had a ridiculous 130 infected people, Italy had a slightly frightening 1,700, and in Switzerland, from where they wanted to depart, the figure was 42.

The virus stated: In all countries, I increased threefold in three days. It went unheard.

Sven and his wife knew about the numbers in China. 2,100 infected people were reported when Ling arrived home on January 27, 36,800 when she returned to Germany head over heels. A day before the start of their dream holiday, it was a staggering 80,000. But now China was far away.

Sven reassured the worried friends and himself: We will fly to New Zealand. A single person is infected there. And if the situation in Germany really escalates, we will stay in New Zealand, after all, we have a visa that is valid for three months.

This ended the rather theoretical discussion. The suitcases were packed quickly, it would start as planned.

Careless Journey

Monday, March 2, 2020

Zurich.

Sven and Ling grouped their suitcases in the S-Bahn so that no one else could find a seat in their area. Also, on the two trains, an IC and an ICE to Zurich, they looked for seats in wagons that were widely empty. They wanted distance. The anti-virus traveled with them and gave good advice, remaining invisible. But on the S-Bahn, which took them from Zurich Central Station to the airport – where they had booked an overnight stay – they could not avoid other people, too many people had the same destination.

From the anti-virus came the good advice: Turn your head aside if someone comes too close to you.

The virus had spread secretly beyond China and was now looking for a new field of activity in Europe. It was prompt: I have already caught more than 2,000 Italians and 40 in Switzerland. Do you really want to return to the bustling city center in the evening? It was annoying. It also unsettled.

They swayed back and forth and still drove for a two-hour city tour into the wet-cold city center of Zurich. The many Asians living there already wore protective masks. During the walk, the virus had no chance to affect their mind and even at night it did not interfere with their sleep.

Tuesday, March 3, 2020

Flight to Singapore.

In the morning, Mr. Neuland and Mrs. Wei took the hotel shuttle to Kloten airport. Ten people of different nationalities sat close together. Only three of them wore a mask.

Virus: I'm flying with you! A short sentence only, but it was enough to describe the situation.

When checking in and later at passport control, their passports were carefully studied. Singapore Airline was well aware that it had to fly anyone who was not allowed to stay in Singapore or in transit back to their airport of departure for free.

Mrs. Wei carried her VIP card from a major Chinese bank. This gave her free access to lounges at airports worldwide, and was also allowed to invite a guest. So, they could have a nice breakfast before going to the gate. Relaxed, they waited for the boarding.

Virus: Do you see the woman over there, how thoroughly she prepares for the flight? It followed them at every turn.

Mr. Neuland turned his head and saw a very attractive woman in her mid-thirties, who celebrated a very special kind of make-up. First, she put on one of the most modern face masks and checked their correct fit several times until she was satisfied with it. She then pulled a pair of goggles out of her LV-bag, and set up the hood of her velvet-soft jacket over her hair. Finally, she donned a pair of long tight-fitting gloves.

Sven Neuland was also able to watch her during the flight. Only when eating and sipping on her champagne glass did she temporarily free herself from her armor. She wasn't the only one wearing a mask. Mrs. Wei did the same, and so did most of the flight attendants. Sven had a mask ready to grip, but saw no need to put it on. During the pleasant flight they forgot the virus, enjoyed the good service and fell into a restful sleep.

Wednesday, March 4, 2020

Flight to Auckland.

The two arrived at Singapore Changi Airport around 6 a.m. Three hours later, the onward flight was scheduled to depart for Auckland.

The virus came out of the blue as they got off the plane: I flew with you. I will be your companion!

They felt it immediately after they left the airplane. Each passenger was diagnosed with a type of laser cannon. Large signs were placed throughout the arrival and transit area, with well over half of the people who were at the airport so early wearing masks.

In the lounge they had a delicious breakfast and showered extensively. As if controlled by an invisible force, Sven took a look at the Corona statistics.

Sven: Already 262 infected in Germany, but thank God only 3 in New Zealand!

Ling: I already know that, and in China only very few new cases have been added. More and more are already healthy again.

Ling used her Chinese app, which showed her the most up-to-date values and lots of graphically processed additional information at all times. In general, she was always a little earlier than her husband when it came to finding out the latest figures.

Three hours later, they were on a plane to Auckland. In addition to Koreans, Chinese were usually among the largest tourist contingents in New Zealand. They often used Singapore as their transit hub. However, as the number of infections in Korea had risen dramatically over the last five days, they too were now affected by an entry ban. This left many seats vacant. They finally arrived in Auckland just before midnight. Fever was measured using the same method as in Singapore. Upon entry, the border policeman studied their travel history very meticulously and at the baggage delivery area a skilled dog sniffs every piece of luggage. This, however, had been part of the arrival in New Zealand for ages and had nothing to do with the virus.

They spent the first night in a hotel near the airport. Twenty-four hours of flight and twelve hours of time difference would not pass without a trace. They were picked up by a hotel shuttle. It was already after midnight when they fell into a restless sleep.

Thursday, March 5, 2020

Flight to Christchurch.

They got up very early and drove without breakfast to the airport. The flight to Christchurch was scheduled to take place at 9:30 a.m. Check-in at the Domestic Terminal was only possible on machines, but they could not read Chinese passports. Therefore, Wei Ling was kindly checked in at the business class counter. Unfortunately, her VIP card was not valid at the domestic lounge, so they bought sandwiches and coffee in a shop in the terminal. That was their barren breakfast. But the stomach hadn't adjusted to the new time zone anyway, so it wasn't possible to tell whether they were hungry or not.

The plane was full. To board the plane stairs were available at the front and rear entrances, so that passengers could get out of the way to some extent while searching their seats. The seats were black, as were the uniforms of the pretty flight attendants. Black is the dominating color in New Zealand. Few passengers wore a mask, there seemed to be normal travel behavior, as ever.

Sven: The virus has certainly overslept the early departure.

Ling: Do you have to think about it every minute? We have holidays.

The view of the mountains of the South Island was phenomenal, a foreboding of the travel experiences that lay in front of them. The airport in Christchurch was very straightforward, but there were also international connections. An Emirates plane and two of Qantas Airways were on the apron.

Sven Neuland was the first to buy a New Zealand SIM card and had no idea that it would be of great use later on. Then they took a taxi to their motel near the city center, where they wanted to stay three nights, acclimatizing. The taxi driver was Korean, had lived here for 15 years and still spoke poor English. They heard from him that the tourism turnover had already collapsed significantly, because his compatriots, but especially no Chinese, were allowed to come. The two also learned that the price level was much higher than in Germany.

Their first route led to the PAK'nSAVE supermarket. It was a kind of Ikea for food.

Anti-virus: Take the disinfectant that hangs on the wall next to the shopping cart. They listened to the good advice.

It took quite a while for them to find in the displays what they wanted to buy as stock for the next few days. Heavily packed, they went the two kilometers back to the motel.

Antivirus: Don't forget to wash hands. Please thoroughly! They promptly followed the request, then put everything in the fridge.

Before falling into a long adjustment sleep, they took a look at their mobile phones.

Virus: I am here, I will be with you all the time now. You will not be able to not think of me for even one day. It stuck like heavy Manuka-honey in their mind.

They read the latest figures from the Corona statistics: 482 in Germany and more than 3,900 in Italy.

Sven wanted to know from the virus: What's going on with Italy?

Virus: They were too reckless and too slow. But this is only the beginning of a major disaster.

The number of new infections in China – which had risen again only slightly – was quickly forgotten. Instead, Korea, and suddenly Iran, came to the fore. The development in New Zealand, on the other hand, did not worry them, as it remained at 3 cases.

Friday, March 6, 2020

Christchurch.

It seemed like a 12-hour jet lag was easier to process than a 7-hour jet lag. The two woke up somewhat fresh. Was there any news from home? Yes, even two. Both of them wanted to bring a few glasses of the famous New Zealand Manuka-honey. Ling explained to Sven what it was all about. Then they made their way to Christchurch city center.

They roamed the huge Hagley-Park, where countless old stately trees towered into the blue sky and provided enough grass for cricket and rugby players. The walkers and joggers spread out in the vastness of the complex, so there was no need for any conscious decision to get out of the way. The park was virus-free. The city center was characterized on the one hand by mostly single-story wooden houses, on the other hand by an almost endless number of gravel parking spaces. Before the great earthquake of 2011, there were houses and office buildings here, people lived here.

Sven: It is very depressing to walk along here.

Ling: Yes, the quake is present at every turn. Look at this church, there is no complete outer wall.

The residents - they spoke to some - took it with them. It has happened and it is now hoped that for a long time we will be spared such strokes of fate, which one is faced with helplessness.

They enjoyed a strong coffee in one of the many street cafés, visited a street food market, a church that had suffered only minor damage, and the memorial to the victims of the earthquake. Then they drank a glass of Chardonnay in the wine cellar of the art museum, in front of which film footage for a commercial was being made. They were allowed to take a quick look into the courtyard of a boys' school where the future elite of New Zealand was trained, it was said on several posters. All students wore a boring dark uniform. The girls in another school opposite were not dressed more briskly. In the evening, Sven brought food out of the Thai restaurant, which was right next to the motel. The deep-seated impression of the destructive power of the earthquake left no room for Corona throughout the day. But before sleep, it has become already a ritual. The Corona statistic showed 4 infected people in New Zealand, so a new case had been added. In Germany, the number of cases became more and more numerous, there were now 670. Further increases were also reported from Korea, Iran and Italy.

Saturday, March 7, 2020

Christchurch.

Again, they went through Hagley-Park to the city center, this time through the southern part. The real cricket fields were laid out here in large numbers. A lot of teams of elite young students had gathered, accompanied by their parents, who used the time for a relaxed chat with each other. The young athletes did not need instructions. Cricket was their weekend job; it was relaxation from daily learning. They wore elegant white clothing and their appearance on the field had something noble, unlike the Kiwis' other cult sport, rugby.

Sven and Ling walked through the beautiful botanical garden, where there were trees that were only native to the area. They reached enormous heights, were often intertwined with other tree trunks like an entire tree family. Tree trunks and branches knew no distances. Those who want to define near, took these trees as an example. The whole complex was the epitome of pure harmony, beauty and security. Next door was the Canterbury Museum, which depicted the history of New Zealand and the region. Both places could be visited without the otherwise often extremely high entrance fees. Sven and Ling learned a lot about the Maori, who came to New Zealand very early. Of course, there were also rooms reserved for the time of British explorers. Ling liked to use her hands to comprehend unfamiliar things. So did the handles of a two-meter-high single wheel that stood in one of the rooms. She had to wait a while until she could climb up. Before her was a tour group of about twenty people, who had the same request. Ling was very amused by the strange vehicle and looked down triumphantly from above on Sven.

Virus: This is an Italian tour group. It had slept for hours, now it suddenly raised the alarm.

Ling: How long have these people been in the country?

Sven: Maybe they only arrived yesterday.

They made a big bow around these people, who were always nearby in all the other rooms. Then they looked for a place to wash their hands thoroughly.

Ling later received a call from the police in her hometown. It wasn't the first. At regular intervals, the local Chinese authorities asked about the well-being of their citizens, even if they were abroad.

In the late afternoon, they took a regular bus to the airport to pick up the rental car, as their round trip was to begin the following day. At each stop, guests disembarked, often students, because the line also served the university area. Each of them thanked the driver loudly as they got out. That was an extraordinary observation. A brightly friendly Hertz-employee took care of the formalities for the rental contract, then Sven got right in the driver's seat, because in New Zealand is driving on the left side of the road. It was a relatively new Toyota Corolla.

After dinner, it was time to send messages to Germany, where the day just started. Sven raved about local lamb and salmon, as well as New Zealand wines, of which he had already tasted three varieties. He also praised the coffee and taste of the fresh milk, but so far, he has not been able to report anything positive for beer.

This was followed by an exchange of information in which, how could it be otherwise, the virus played the decisive role. Sven noticed in the daily study of the statistics that consistent case numbers were reported by most countries in the various media. For Germany, on the other hand, this was not the case. The figures from the Robert Koch Institute (RKI) differed greatly from those of the World Health Organization (WHO). The highest values were regularly reported by Johns Hopkins University (JHU). Some press bodies in Germany even managed to present different figures in the same article. Did it make a difference whether 792 or 813 people are infected? Sven thought that was very important. He also found recommendations by individual German politicians that people should avoid strolling around certain regions or even cities.

Sven to his friends: Do you heed this advice?

Friend-1: No.

Friend-2: Why? There is no death case in Germany yet because of Corona.

This was more than surprising, as in Italy the number of Corona deaths was already 5% of those infected. That was the highest percentage rate in the world. Here in New Zealand, the number remained constant at 5 infected. No reason for an unquiet night.

Sunday, March 8, 2020

Omarama.

After breakfast, they left Christchurch, not without first shopping at the PAK'nSAVE supermarket. They would come through numerous small towns where there are probably no shops. Therefore, they bought a small stock for two to three days. In addition to the usual food, the first glass of the famous Manuka-honey also landed in the shopping cart. It was, of course, an inexpensive variety, because the ones with the best quality were not to be found in the supermarkets.

It was cool and it was raining lightly again and again. The journey went more than half an hour through suburbs of Christchurch, towards the south-west. Then it became empty on the road, the landscape was more impressive and first large flocks of sheep and cattle grazed peacefully in the lush greenery on extensive meadows to the left and right of the state highway. Around noon, they reached Lake Tekapo. In a Japanese restaurant, they ate a bad-tasting pasta dish, then walked to the shore of the huge lake, where there were no boats to be seen. The water was clear and glacier-green. The path led over a swinging bridge to a small chapel, where a businesswoman with s strict view watched over the fact that no one took a photo in the interior without throwing an obolus into a bowl. A little further away stood a monument of a shepherd, which was mainly dedicated to his herd dog, who had always supported him in his work to the best of his ability. After a good two hours on the lake, which is not overcrowded by tourists today, they drove another hour to the present destination, the Ahuriri Motel in Omarama. It borrowed the name of the river that crossed the place.

Omarama was a hicktown. It had only two streets, a gas station, a small grocery store and two restaurants. One of them was open. All the people who were hungry or just looking for a chat with others met there in the evening. The pub was well filled. Sven and Ling ordered lamb, fish and two large beers. As almost everywhere, you had to go to the counter and place the order there. They paid immediately and received a wooden box with a number inserted into it. They clearly placed it on the table and waited for the food to be brought. It tasted excellent.

The vast majority of the guests were New Zealanders, wherever they came from. Many knew each other. The locals chatted at rustic volume across the room. Many had appeared in ancient clothes, some barefoot, and outwardness were not taken into account. TV-sets hung on the wall on all sides of the restaurant. There were rugby matches on show and many stared at the players, who rush at the player with the egg-shaped ball.

As they walked back to the motel, they roamed two streets with stately wooden houses in large gardens. People didn't meet them. At the motel, they came back with the word Corona.

Virus: Finally turn on your mobile phones, don't you want to know how I spread? There wasn't a day when it didn't control their thoughts at least once.

Of course, they wanted to know, reached for the mobile phones and opened the German and Chinese app with the latest statistics.

Virus: You see, in your homeland I have already caught more than 1,000 people not to talk about what I am doing in Italy. It managed to get the two worried.

Anti-virus: Be reassured, here in New Zealand it hasn't happened anymore, still only 5. No need to worry. The debate between the two was still in balance.

More confusing were the messages that friends from Germany posted on WhatsApp. Apparently, there was a kind of panic. Just a few days ago it was said that Corona would not be an issue for us, that we were well prepared. Suddenly, however, virologists appeared on all TV channels, who took a very different view. One of her central findings was communicated to the people by the Chancellor, who had so far been noticed by her consistent silence throughout the matter. Immediately, it was assumed that there is a permanent threat which could only be defeated if 60 to 70 percent of the population became infected and thus became immune. What a gigantic number and how do you know that after the infestation with the virus and the cure, immunity will undoubtedly occur? The whole thing should be magically stretched over a period of 2 years or more.

Sven was so far away from Germany that he noticed it, but did not let it distract him from sleep. There had already been a change of strategy in Germany from just afterwards on other occasions.

Monday, March 9, 2020

Dunedin.

The morning was cool, the clouds hung low and made the first kilometers on the empty road a ghost ride. As if through an opening veil, with which the wind played, a mountain ridge from the white-grey appeared from time to time. The road was wide and led along several lakes to the east coast. The fog cleared for a few seconds, without notice, in order to immediately limit the view to 20 meters.

Sven and Ling came to a place where rock drawings of the Maori could be seen. It took some imagination and good eyes to really recognize them. More impressive was the formation of the stone layers that these drawings were in them. After a good hour the sun came out, it quickly warmed up and the clouds dissolved, the fog was extinguished. At one of the lakes, they made a walk along a path along an avenue of thick trees. In their branch work, spiders had artfully and precisely stretched their enormous webs. Two old men lined a boat to catch some fish for personal use. The calm with which they did their work has something sublime.

Then they reached Oamaru and saw the South Pacific for the first time. The visit to the colony of blue penguins was not worthwhile at this time of day, as all the animals in the sea romped to catch fish. A whole bunch of lazy seals had laid down on the rocks for sunbathing. That was worth an observation. The surf was extremely strong, it washed a lot of tang and driftwood to the shore and thus also the typical smell of the sea. Afterwards, they took a quick look at Oamaru's old streets with the colonial buildings, where not so long ago there was a lot of activity. Today the place was extinct. They only looked at the quirky Steampunk Museum from the outside. An old steam locomotive stood in front of the entrance, pointing slightly obliquely upwards, and every 15 minutes it swelled and thrust white steam into the blue sky.

On the way south they found a beautiful garden café. They sat outside under a tree, in the middle of a flower garden, ate fish and chips and a heavy English muffin, then drove on to Moeraki-Boulders Beach.

The path to the large ball-shaped stones led through the dunes down to the water edge. It was flood. You could walk a few hundred meters along the beach, over stones and driftwood, get wet feet again and again or, like Ling in her euphoria, fell straight into the mud. Due to the flood, the stone balls did not seem as impressive as expected, because not even the whole upper half could be seen. Once back at the parking lot, cleaning equipment was ready to clean the shoes covered in mud. They took another walk-through dense forest, where low trees stood and the undergrowth was impenetrable. From here they had an impressive view of the deep sea, whose grey color was only lighter by nuances than that of the stones. A third shade of grey was provided by the sky. So, the eyes saw three variants of grey, otherwise no other colors.

Finally, they reached their accommodation in Dunedin in the evening. The Adrian Motel was very close to the sea, but it had started to rain again and the planned beach walk was therefore cancelled. They drove off to find something to eat nearby. Ultimately, they opted for one of several China take-aways. It was the wrong decision. The routine view of the Corona statistic did not touch them any further. Still constant 5 infected in New Zealand and just over 1,200 in Germany. No need to worry about where they were now, they were safe.

Tuesday, March 10, 2020

Te Anau.

Today's goal was far to the west. But first a short detour to the Otago Peninsula was planned, on which is the only castle in New Zealand, Larnach-Castle. The fog was even denser than the day before, almost impenetrable. Already far in front of the castle garden stood the ticket office. For the visit of the park and some rooms, the tickets had to be purchased here. In this weather, it is a completely pointless spending. The roads on the peninsula were narrow and winding, so it took quite a while for Mr. Neuland and Mrs. Wei to arrive back in Dunedin. They stopped to visit the famous train station, a truly stately building that they never expected in this remote place. They then drove south for a while, towards Invercargill. There was heavy traffic, with numerous trucks supplying goods to the southernmost towns of New Zealand. For an hour the ride was uninteresting, hardly anything worth seeing was on the eye.

   In the small village of Gore, it turned towards a narrower road that led slightly northwest to Te Anau. Mountains, green slopes, wide valleys as far as you could see. A mixture of Tyrol and Allgäu in Germany, only the air was cleaner, even clinically pure. The road was poorly trafficked and yet Te Anau was unexpectedly full. All the tourism in this area was in this place, the starting point for the exploration of the Fjordland National Park and, of course, the Milford Sound. After a short search, they found a big supermarket, then checked into the Anchorage Motel apartments. It was a normal motel; the car could be parked right outside the door. They got a small bottle of fresh milk again. At the reception, they were told that you were not allowed to drive your own car to Milford Sound at the moment. There would only be the possibility of an organized bus ride from Te Anau. It would last a whole day. Later, Sven Neuland inquired at the Visitor Information Center, where this information was confirmed. It was only after two questions that he was informed that most of the Milford Highway was easily allowed to be driven by his own car, only the last few kilometers to the sound were not. They decided against the bus, thus also against the alleged climax of this area, the Milford sound. To be driven from vantage point to vantage point for hours in the middle of a 40-strong tour group, only to be spit out at the Milford Sound at the same time after a block clearance from one of a hundred buses at the same time, did not sound very tempting.

In the evening there was a choice between several restaurants, all of which were full. In a very appealing-looking grill restaurant, they put themselves on the waiting list and ordered a cool beer to bridge the announced 15 minutes of waiting time. The professional service knew how to catch customers. After 30 minutes, they still didn't have a table. They went and returned to a half-empty pizzeria. The quality of the food was not even mediocre. As in no other place before, it became abundantly clear that in Te Anau it was very good to take as much money out of the tourists' pockets as possible.

In the evening, they casually devoted a few minutes to the virus. Ling's Chinese app also named the number 5 for New Zealand. A paradise of security. In Germany, on the other hand, things quickly continued to rise. More than 1,500 infected people were already registered. But it was still reported in the press that Corona would not have a major impact on

Mr. Neuland's home country. Spain was close to Germany. We had to keep an eye on the south of Europe. News from friends at home had not arrived. There was obviously nothing important to say.

Wednesday, March 11, 2020

Te Anau.

Sven and Ling packed food into the car for a day, because there would be no refreshment on the way. The Milford Highway led first along Lake Te Anau and then deeper and deeper into an imposing mountain world. On the road they found numerous vantage points where they stopped. Small lakes lay quietly in the middle of the imposing mountains. Water flowed everywhere and large plains were overgrown with high gold-yellow grass. These were the places where the tourist buses spit out hundreds of people for 10 minutes and let them jump around there completely losing their inhibitions. Photos were taken of people standing in the grass, squatting, lying down. Videos were made of people jumping through the meadow. More and more buses were heading west to arrive at the point where they were allowed to continue twice a day in a block check-in to Milford Sound. So, dozens of buses close behind each other. During the rest of the time, the road was repaired.

After 100 kilometers, Sven and Ling finished their journey. A friendly ranger explained what they already knew. They were allowed to park their car and were able to take a long walk. They enjoyed great views of the mountains, which are more than 2,500 meters high, and discovered some strange birds in the foliage, whose melodic singing gave life to silence. Milford didn't see them, but they didn't regret it either.

On the way back, they made a stop at Lake Gunn. There was a hiking trail through the enchanted fairy-tale forest, which led them for over an hour through a land of fairies, goblins, giants and other mystical beings. So, this was the land in which the film "Lord of the Rings" was shot. If you were to walk here at night or at dusk, the fear would be a constant companion. In the evening, they strolled along the shores of the lake, near the town center, and then fried an excellent-tasting fish in their motel. The day ended with a glass or two of wine.

Virus: Stop! More clearly than all the days before, this devil was back on the spot. Put your glasses aside, it's time to get restless.

The virus was right. A lot of information bounced out of the phone and swirled the tired brain cells of the saturated bodies. The numbers of the countries they focused on knew only one way up. 1,900 infected in Germany, 12,500 in Italy, over 2,000 in Spain, 21,000 in Iran, 7,800 in Korea. What a trend! But New Zealand kept the rock in the surf. There were no more, still only 5. They felt safe and free. If the situation in Europe were to escalate, Sven thought, they would stay in New Zealand for a few weeks longer, after all, their visa was valid until the end of May. It was almost impossible to get reliable current figures from the German media, and the sources to which the press referred were too different. The death rate in Italy was rapidly approaching that of China. Those responsible at the most diverse federal levels in Germany always issued new regulations or recommendations. Suddenly, assembly bans for more than 500 participants were discussed in one province, while in another the figure was 2,000. Italians still did not wear masks and many did not take house arrest seriously. Four weeks ago, Ling came back to Germany in panic because there were 65! People infected there. Now even Germany had more of it than any single Chinese province except Hubei. China had already shut down and sealed off the country completely six weeks ago, completely banning movements and social contacts. Incredible capacities of medical facilities were knocked out of the ground with great force and all Chinese, without exception, wore a mask. It seemed to be a success when you looked at the Chinese numbers. In Germany, nothing of the sort has still been ordered. Chaos, uncertainty, and ignorance seemed to guide the decision-makers. For the first time, Sven and Ling wondered whether it was wise to return to Germany on April 10 as planned. By then, more than 100,000 people could be infected there as well. It was the first evening of their trip, when they not only read the latest figures, but also thought about which scenarios might soon arise and which decisions would have to be made in person.

Thursday, March 12, 2020

Queenstown.

They left Te Anau after breakfast, more specifically after the first half of the Champions League match between Liverpool and Atlético Madrid. It looked good for the Reds.

Virus: Do you see that the stadium is filled to the last seat? Why did it bother Sven's football enjoyment in the morning?

Virus: You will see the consequences. Also, in Leipzig and other places, I invited tens of thousands to make acquaintance with me in the stadium.

Sven knew this and was surprised that some stadiums were full, while other games took place in front of empty ranks. After all, there was the EU, UEFA. Why could these institutions not legislate uniform rules across Europe?

It was only 180 kilometers to Queenstown, but they took three hours, because there were so many places on the way where it was worth getting off. They found the snake-shaped

Lake Wakatipu a pearl among the natural beauties of New Zealand.

Their motel had already gotten a bit old, but it was well-located and offered direct views of the lake. It was run by Indians. They were able to check in as early as 1 p.m. First, they took a walk along the lakeshore to the small city center, which was full of cafés, bars, restaurants and people. The afternoon cocktail or cappuccino there was an exuberant atmosphere. Queenstown was the melting pot of the South Island. Elegant ladies and gentlemen in business outfits mingled with backpackers who sat on the lake shore with a bottle of wine in hand and long-time no washed trousers. The two considered whether to climb to Ben Lomond on foot, but chose the cable car, which had been built by the Austrian company Doppelmayr.

The local mountain of Queenstown was an Eldorado for leisure, a brilliant excursion destination. It began with a beautiful panoramic view of the city, the lake and the New Zealand Southern Alps. Upstairs, two intertwined go-kart tracks had been laid out, on which not only the little ones romped. There were several mountain bikes routes and a departure point for paragliders. The staff prepared each flight with great care and composure. Finally, they strapped the daredevil people to their belly and floated with them in wide arcs into the depths. Among the brave ones were a young Taiwanese couple and a Kiwi pensioner who had clearly exceeded her 70th. For the descent Sven and Ling chose the steep footpath. It led through the middle of the forest. Few of them were on the road here. Below, the path ended next to the cemetery, where the graves were filled with a striking number of flowers.

Back in the city, they found a table in a beautiful restaurant in the overcrowded pedestrian zone. There was fish and lamb, along with a local beer from a micro-brewery on their table.

Sven: Where do most of the people who are in Queenstown come from?

Waiter: Oh, these are mainly Kiwis from the North Island. In addition, Europeans and Americans, but also Indians. Chinese and Koreans are currently missing. You know, because of the virus. And then there are many South Americans here, but not as tourists, but as helpers in the pubs, restaurants and hotels.

They went back to the motel. The day was exhausting and the legs demanded recreation.

Virus: Sven, think of the evening routine! Look at what I did while you forgot me all day long.

Looking at the Corona statistics had become an everyday routine for Sven and Ling. As always in the last few days, there were still a reassuring 5 infected people in New Zealand, but more than 2,100 in Germany. Sven read to his astonishment that local authorities have so far provided the RKI with the figures both mechanically and manually. Manually? He couldn't believe it. Today, the RKI informed that manually transmitted data would no longer be accepted. As a result, the numbers of cases would inevitably have to decrease the following day, Sven thought. He studied some numbers from other European countries, but forgot them again after a minute. Korea seemed to have the situation under control, China anyway.

Friday, March 13, 2020

Wanaka.

During the night, Sven and Ling had stopped working on the virus. Every day they felt how infinitely far away Germany was. They first drove 30 kilometers northwest to Glenorchy. The small village was located at the end of Lake Wakatipu. Here some sections of the film "Lord of the Rings" were shot. The Wetland-Trail was particularly beautiful. On wooden planks, which were covered with wire mesh to avoid slipping, they walked for an hour over swampy terrain, along shallow water surfaces, on which a large number of black majestic swans made their way. Sven refueled the car, because on some routes, even today, there would be no gas station for more than 100 kilometers. Therefore, refilling should not be waited too long. The scenery was fantastic. Mountains, valleys, clean air, crystal clear lakes wherever they looked.

On their way to Gibbston, they passed the legendary AJ Hackett Kawarau Bungy Jumping Center. There was a lot of hustle and bustle of onlookers and daring people. A large visitor center had been built in which one was prepared for the jump with hot beats. In the middle of the bridge was the jumping point. As they watched in amazement, a young Spanish girl jumped first and then a 10-year-old boy. It wasn't his first jump. After the rope had calmed down, the jumpers were lowered to the surface of the water, where they were picked up by a crew with an inflatable boat.

A few kilometers further on, they visited one of the numerous wineries. It was set in a magnificent basin, had a cozy garden restaurant in the shade and a cheese factory where they took a snack and tasted a glass of the Pinot Gris grown here.

In the afternoon they reached Wanaka. It was hard to get a room at all. Why was everything booked out here? When they arrived, they knew the reason. This weekend, the Wanaka Farmers Market took place. They stayed in a nice room of a hostel, shopped at the New World supermarket and then walked across the Farmers Market between tractors, lawnmowers, horses and all sorts of agricultural equipment. It was actually already closed, but the gates were open. At the very end of the big square it was loud and crowded. There the exhibitors had gathered for canned beer and hot dogs. Sven and Ling stopped on the edge with their sausage.

Virus: Are you afraid of the turmoil?

Ling: Yes, a little bit. Satisfied, the virus heard her response.

It was this time when there were always thoughts about whether too large crowds should perhaps be avoided better. A walk along the magnificent Lake Wanaka concluded the day.

Later in the evening, the silent dialogue with the virus began again. As if set in stone, the number 5 stood for New Zealand, while in Germany there was a large increase to 3,700 cases. The news from home was the most important thing: everyone was healthy. But they also learned that the population was becoming increasingly restless. The word "panic buying" fell more often, in many supermarkets were (temporarily?) toilet paper, noodles, canned food and soap sold out. Many companies have taken various preventive measures since a few days, closed canteens, issued travel bans, canceled events, and began working in the home office. The streets are still full, he read, but Corona has become a central issue in the country. So, they were in good hands at the other end of the world, Sven was sure, as the stars glowed brightly and brightly over the lake.

Saturday, March 14, 2020

Fox Glacier.

Today, a long drive to the west coast was on the agenda. They took all the time in the world and enjoyed the views of water, mountains and lush meadows. There was little traffic. They stopped at the Blue-Pools. From the parking lot, a hiking trail led to an azure lake. Impressive was the long swinging bridge, which Sven crossed extremely carefully, while Ling danced light-footed and without fear over it.

Then they reached the Tasman Sea, which is located between New Zealand and Australia. The sea was rough, the beaches invited for a walk, but not for sunbathing. They were full of driftwood, tree trunks and branches. At a vantage point stood a wooden tower, from which one could look far over the sea. Eventually, they arrived at Fox Glacier, a tiny place in the immediate vicinity of New Zealand's two highest mountains, Mount Tasman and Mount Cook.

Their motel was about two kilometers from the main road, where there were three restaurants, a small shop and a refueling station. Most of the rooms were free, only four other vehicles were standing on the parking lot. They had a magnificent garden behind their apartment and could look at the two mountains from which the clouds dissolved in the late afternoon. In the evening they cooked chicken meat, there was nothing else to buy in the supermarket today. The virus did not interfere with the relaxed end of the day. A new case had been added in New Zealand, there were now 6 infected. In Germany, 4,600 were reported as infected.

Sunday, March 15, 2020

Fox Glacier.

Virus: Have you finally woken up? The question roared into Sven's ears. There had to be a special reason for this. Sven opened WhatsApp and read some things that seemed disturbing. A friend informed him that New Zealand would prohibit all entry from Germany from March 16. The rapid increase in the number of people infected in Europe has now been noted worldwide. New Zealand reacted quickly, which should be even more impressive later on.

Sven: Don't bother us, because we're already there! He wrote the answer in a flap. He asked if all activities outside the apartment had been stopped at home. That was denied.

Friend-1: We reduce our social contacts, but all the restaurants and shops are still open.

Friend-3: A rumor makes the rounds. Germany will soon close all borders.

Friend-2: Schools, day care centers, theatres, swimming pools and other facilities are already closed. Events have been cancelled, flights can be rebooked or cancelled more flexibly than ever before.

Friend-3: Not to forget: Football is no longer played.

For many compatriots, the latter seemed to be the greatest possible limitation of all. The list of what was unthinkable two weeks ago continued with the following messages:

Germans are already not allowed to enter 30 countries.

In the Maldives, 100 German tourists were stranded and did not know how to return, because both entry and departure were prohibited there.

The ski season in Tyrol is also over.

On the part of the German Chancellor, as is so often the case, there would only be an appeal for social contacts to be reduced to a minimum.

The virologists, to whom the government listened, agreed that the virus could no longer be captured.

A strategy that was surprising to Sven became the maxim of political action overnight: herd immunity. Within two years, perhaps a little more, 70% of the population should become infected. In the survivors, this would create permanent immunity and thus eradicate the virus. Sven calculated: Germany has 83 million inhabitants. 70% of this is 58 million. Evenly distributed over two years which is 730 days, this means more than 76,000 new infections per day. Well then good luck with this strategy.

After breakfast, he had parked this information in his brain in such a way that it could not affect the day. They drove the short distance to the parking lot, from where the hiking trails started in the direction of Fox Glacier. Because of the high-water level in the riverbed, through parts of the path passed, they did not come as close to the glacier as at times with normal water levels. But the very path that the hour-long hike took was fascinating. It passed through a jungle. Is there another place on this earth where jungles and high mountains are so close to each other? Each tree had its own quirky shape, the forest was impenetrable beyond the paths. It radiated total calm. There were no insects, no snakes, no wild, dangerous animals. There was only peaceful harmonic nature, if it had not been for the endless chain of helicopters that flew the short-time tours around the glacier in 20 minutes. One followed the other, the noise of the rotors disturbed the nature experience very much, but it brought the land revenue that it desperately needed. The glacier itself, as expected, no longer looked very spectacular. Over the decades, it had shrunk enormously. On the hike, they tried again and again to keep a 2-metre distance from the oncoming. Why did they do that? Others were much more relaxed. Sven and Ling already took what was soon to become the official requirement. For the way back, they chose a narrower path, the Moraine-Walk, which led even deeper through the jungle.

In the late afternoon, they circled Lake Matheson. In its water, the mountains should be particularly intensely reflected when it was windless and it did not curl. At the beginning of the trail there was a fantastic café and an oversized red wooden frame. It had been placed at the point from which the photos with the white mountain peaks in the background would be best. Unfortunately, the water was a bit restless, so they did not experience the perfect mirror image, but both peaks were cloud-free, which was not the case every day. At this time of day many people came here, also some tour groups from India and Italy. Italy! This urged caution. The distance was extended over 2 meters.

In the evening, they dined in one of the restaurants, which was decorated like an American saloon. In the interior, every table was occupied, but there were free seats on the terrace. They ordered indoors at the counter and soon after a tasty meal stood on the heavy wooden table. They sat on bar stools with fish and chips, lamb and roast potatoes, along with freshly tapped ale. A comfortable place in an atmospheric ambience.

Virus: There are more and more, it is time to get worried.

It was again the uninvited guest who disturbed the evening rest in the garden. Sven looked up. Two more cases were added today in New Zealand. In Germany, the number had risen to 5,800. What was going on with the US? No 3,000 cases. Congratulations! The virus couldn't harm this country either. What a fallacy, but that was just a foreboding today.

Monday, March 16, 2020

Hokitika.

During the night, cloudbursts fell for hours. The rain drummed against the windows and on the roof. Sven woke up to it.

Virus: Use the early hour and switch on your phone. I have done a lot of new things.

Sven responded to the call and read that public life in Germany had come to a standstill, that there were no more cultural or sporting events, that schools and kindergartens were closed. He asked the friends if it was advisable to come back as planned or better stay a few weeks longer in New Zealand? The answers were received without hesitation.

Friend-1: Extend, no question!

Friend-2: Stay in New Zealand!

Friend-3: Why do you ask, of course stay there!

A smorgasbord of thoughts formed in his brain and flowed into the keyboard at an early hour:

Why could we not define in a uniform way what a major event is?

Why could empty halls not be converted into temporary hospitals?

Why was it not possible to use the federal armed forces to support medical measures?

Why were masks still considered completely useless?

Why didn't we at least create consistent communication?

Why were there still some ice cream parlors and cafés full of people who wanted to enjoy the spring weather without restrictions?

Sven also read about measures of even greater significance: the first border closures had been ordered. It concerned France, Austria, Switzerland and Denmark. What dynamic force had changed life at home in just 14 days?

For breakfast, these developments were again a long way off, as a new eventful day lay ahead of the two travelers. In the morning it was windless. Ideal to go to Lake Matheson again. The light for taking photos was a thousand times better than last evening, so all the snapshots were taken again and the one deleted from yesterday. They circled the lake only partially, but they found the places of the perfect mirror image.

Then they went on to the neighboring village Franz Josef. There was the second formerly large glacier. The hiking trail there was much wider than the one at the Fox Glacier, because here the bus caravans arrived and spit out their passengers towards the ice field. Huge avalanches of debris, which had smashed wide lanes into the steep slopes and left only skeletons of broken trees, shaped this path.

It was lined with a handful of narrow but very high waterfalls. They only saw the glacier from a distance. There were three cleverly placed viewpoints on it. The majesty of bygone times was gone. In addition, a light grey veil had been placed on the ice. Jacinda Ardern, New Zealand's Prime Minister, therefore blamed the Australian wildfires of recent months, they learned from a connoisseur of the political situation. In general, the relationship between the two countries would not be particularly the best.

Their journey continued north. Along the way there were a few places where a hundred years ago a successful search for gold was sought. The village of Ross was one of several small gold mining places that invited you to take a walk. On the way, the mountains sometimes retreated far into the hinterland to allow sheep and cattle breeding on endless meadows. A large group of several hundred cows moved along a narrow path of leisurely steps towards a place where they were freed from the contents of their bulging udders. As on almost all roads, repair work was constantly underway. Traffic lights were only needed in the rarest of cases. A mostly wild-looking beard-wearing man held the stop-go sign and turned it on the right side in consultation with his colleague at the other end of the construction site. At Green, he elegantly swinging his free hand towards each vehicle, with four spread fingers ultimately making up the actual greeting.

They reached their destination Hokitika in the early afternoon. The lodge was located directly on the sea. They moved into a dreamlike wooden house. Just below the terrace was the beach. Time and space to the muse.

When checking in, the virus spoke through the woman's mouth at the reception: Please read this questionnaire carefully about your health and fill it out in full, only then may I give you the key. It was the first time they experienced Corona in a formal way.

They shopped at the well-stocked New-World supermarket and spent the rest of the day in their wooden house. They experienced the sunset together with some others directly on the beach. Three spotlessly clean alpacas grazed inside the complex. When it got dark, they walked a hundred meters up the mountain into a forest across the street. In fact, it glowed everywhere in the trees and on the shrubs. Millions of fireflies enchanted the night. The eight to ten other visitors all whispered, although loud speech would not harm the ritual. Whispers, however, fitted much better with this spectacle.

The habit of comparing numbers did not end tonight either. In addition, 8 cases were reported for New Zealand. Was it appropriate to use such questionnaires already now?

Tuesday, 17. March 2020

Oven River.

Virus: Wake up, there's definitely news for you!

Why was this stupid virus so penetrating every day after waking up?

Virus: During the New Zealand night, the old day in Germany came to an end and you certainly are worried that there is depressing news.

The virus was right. Curious and restless, Sven took his mobile phone, still in half-sleep he read line by line the further enriched list of restrictions in Germany.

From today, theatres, saunas, swimming pools, clubs and discos remained closed.

Public traffic at banks and the public sector has been severely restricted.

All the North Sea and Baltic Sea islands were closed for tourists, those who were still there had to leave the islands immediately. Due to the lockdown in many other European countries (Spain, Italy, Austria, France, Denmark) many had travelled to the German coast for a spontaneous Corona holiday.

Sven could not give a final answer to the question of when they would finally return. He read that more and more airlines had completely suspended operations from one day to the next. He really couldn't predict what it would look like on their flight in three weeks at the moment. For all the normality that another friend still thought he was watching, he still felt that more and more people were becoming more cautious and keeping bigger distances at the supermarket cash registers.

They didn't let all these upsets spoil their breakfast. Overlooking the sea, they used the wooden terrace for a sumptuous meal. Then they continued their journey. They drove a good distance north, along the coast, to Shanty Town. An old gold-digger village had been preserved there, the center of which had been restored in a very impressive way. A worthwhile stay. They walked through the two village streets, looked into a bakery, visited the small church, a newspaper printing house, also the prison, which had only two narrow cells, a pub and many other shops. Inside, they were all lovingly equipped with old utensils. So that's what life looked like in the gold mining era. Of course, it was only reserved for the successful miners to spend their just won money here again. An event was prepared in the large festival hall in which the dairy industry would hand over its awards and orders tomorrow. Tables were lined up close together, the stage decorated, the dance floor prepared. There would be no 2-metre distance here. But it should also be a good week before the two became the magic number in New Zealand. With a hundred-year-old steam locomotive and two not-younger wagons, they made a short journey, which took them a bit far into the mountains at a snail's pace. There were the gold mines. The locomotive was simmering, jerking and steaming. Those who paid a few dollars extra were also allowed to look for gold with a pan, a find was guaranteed.

The Pancake-Rocks were very spectacular, just 50 kilometers further north. It was an extremely interesting geological formation of densely stacked extreme flat rock discs. The sea had drilled through it in several places and roared through the huge holes with enormous surf. The New Zealanders were able to create the hiking trail in such a way that you could really enjoy the most spectacular views.

Eventually they turned east, left the Tasman Sea and drove through vast forests, from which large areas had been cleared and some of them had just been reforested. In the middle of the 100-kilometer long route was the "Berlin" rest house, an opportunity to strengthen themselves with fish and beef burgers.

Their very simple motel, operated by a Chinese couple, was located directly on the road, where a few trucks were also on the way at night. During the day, cats or similarly large animals were often seen lying on the road, which had been run over during the night. No one cleared them. There were enough birds to do this in a few days.

Virus: There are 12!

Sven: What's the point, only 4 more than yesterday, that's nothing.

Virus: It's 50% more than yesterday!

Too many numbers, too much occasions for interpretation. Nevertheless, Sven took another look at Germany. 9,300 people were reported infected. It seemed that the strict measures had waited too long.

Wednesday, March 18, 2020

Pohara.

Breakfast in their small uncomfortable room didn't take much time, then they were on their way back to their next destination. The night was cold, the heating was not working properly. That's why the Corona virus was not visible this morning. Of course, it made up leeway in the afternoon.

They made a first stop in Motueka and walked along the main road. Nothing special, no reason for a longer break. Along the way, they crossed large fruit growing areas, especially apples and pears grew here. Then they tormented themselves in endless bends up the Takaka Pass. On the route there was a kilometer-long construction site, at whose traffic lights they had to wait for 15 minutes. On the top was a beautiful path, from the end of which they had a wide view of the Abel Tasman National Park and the sea to the front of Nelson.

When they arrived in Pohara, the motel's reception was not yet occupied. They drove a few kilometers by the sea and then went to the small General Store to buy something to eat. There was a lot of fish, but most of the offer was pre-ordered, the name of the customers was on the glued labels. After checking into a beautiful apartment with a direct view of the sea, they took an extensive walk along the beach, on which long waves rolled on the sand. Upstairs stood some stately villas, downstairs a few locals let their dogs run. The freshly prepared fish tasted excellent and the wine as well. On the balcony table, dozens of shells that Ling had collected dried.

Virus: It's time to get involved with me!

Sven: Disappear!

Virus: That's not how you talk to me. Too much has happened, you will have to change your plans soon. I will not allow your journey to continue so carefree.

Unfortunately, the virus was right, because what Sven read did not sound good.

The numbers in Italy were alarmingly high, with Germany and France leading a head-to-head race for a place in the top ten countries with the most infected people. The eye swiped the number for New Zealand. It had risen to 20, from 12. There was something in the air. In Germany, they had now reached 12,300.

Sven: No cause for concern.

Virus: But do you still think that you can fly to Zurich as planned and take the train to Germany from there?

In addition to the information extracted from the media, other updates arrived from the friends. At the staccato pace, the lines flew past his eyes:

Entry ban for non-EU citizens.

Closed airports, cancelled flights, hardly any new flights.

The society was slowed down to zero, in many countries the entry for Germans was already forbidden.

Hopefully New Zealand wouldn't also become a crisis zone and then expel all the strangers from the country. That didn't sound relaxed anymore. In Sven's place of residence in Germany, the first case of infection had been confirmed.

The entry ban for non-EU citizens was a message that directly affected Sven and Ling. He asked anxiously and asked for clarification, which also arrived promptly. The entry ban does not apply to Ling because she has a long-term residence permit for Germany. That is one of the few exceptions. This reassured Sven, but he suspected a problem that had to be solved, at least mitigated. Ling's residence permit had been approved four weeks ago, but she had not received the eAT, the real document, before the trip. Sven had, after all, taken copies of important documents with him. On the one hand, a letter from the immigration authority and, on the other hand, the proof of payment for the issuance of the eAT. Would that be enough for the Federal Police when entering Frankfurt airport? They would be in Wellington next Monday. They planned to go to the embassy there to get some suitable replacement document for the eAT.

He later learned that they had to cancel the planned stopover in Qatar because Qatar had also banned entry for all foreigners. Finally, another message was received, which could later become relevant: The Foreign Office wanted to launch a worldwide return campaign of German citizens who are abroad. For this purpose, it has set up a website on which you should register if you wish to be included in the program. It bore the beautiful name ELEFAND (Electronic Registration of Germans Abroad). Today's attempt to get involved failed because the site was unreachable. Some technical problem. Well, then tomorrow.

Thursday, March 19, 2020

Picton.

Before breakfast, Sven called Qatar Airways. He got good news. At first, he was confirmed that Qatar would continue to allow transit in Doha without restriction, and he was also assured that there were currently no plans to cease operations right now. Anyway. He was able to rebook the flight home. Now, after transit in Doha, they would fly directly to Frankfurt and no longer via Zurich. This brought a bit of certainty to their planning.

While Ling was preparing breakfast, Sven was still busy with his mobile phone. Read notifications, write answers, ask questions. The family was fine, everyone was healthy. One of his nephews, a teacher, tried more than badly to continue teaching by e-mail. Another nephew was sitting in the home office for the foreseeable future. Sven again called up the crisis preparedness list of the Federal Republic of Germany. This time it succeeded and he registered himself and Ling. A minute later, the Foreign Office confirmed by e-mail that they had successfully registered in ELEFAND.

Friend-1: The test sets have run out in Stuttgart.

Friend-3: On the Zugspitze, skiers crowd despite the ban and official end of the ski season.

Friend-2 adds: Talk shows and other shows take place without viewers.

Before breakfast, he listened to the chancellor's speech to the nation: the situation was very worrying, but not serious enough for a complete lockdown, she said. People should keep even more distance from each other, in general, it is the citizens who held everything in their own hands.

Friend-1 commented: In other words, if things go wrong, it is the citizens' fault, not the responsibility of the government.

Sven: I was particularly impressed by her suggestion that grandchildren should write letters to their grandparents again, because the mail will continue to be delivered by the Post Office. She gave impressive advice on how digital power Germany could shape virtual communication. That had reassured him a lot.

They enjoyed their breakfast overlooking the sea in their motel in the lonely Pohara. Only two other vehicles were parked in the parking lot. The journey towards Picton went half an hour through flat rising farmland. Almost no other car was on the road. The road climbed steadily to the Takaka Pass, which they crossed this time from the other side. They came back through Motueka and then turned north before Nelson. Suddenly, the road that often ran along the sea was full of trucks. They came from the ferry ports and brought supplies from the North Island. In Nelson, they gave up a stop, but got off in Havelock. A small town at the end of a bay of a fjord. Hundreds of sailing yachts anchored here. There were a few restaurants. In one they ordered Fish & Chips. After the meal had been freshly prepared, the head of the house brought the cargo outside, where they waited at a wooden table. He placed a huge bundle wrapped in thick paper in front of them. They barely managed half. They took the other half to the car for the evening.

Instead of the main road, they drove along a winding side road to Picton. Again, there were magnificent views of the fjords. They saw huge mountain slopes with no tree left, everything had been cleared. Shortly before Picton, there was a path from which they could watch the incoming and outgoing ships of the Bluebridge and Interislander Cook Strait Ferry. A nice spectacle, because both one ship just departed and another arrived.

Sven: Hey, Corona virus, where are you this afternoon?

Sven was quite relaxed, but already when checking in at the hotel in the city center, it came back.

Virus: Please complete this health questionnaire. One sheet per person.

They already knew the questions from Hokitika.

Virus: Please also the back side.

The sheet was more extensive. The arrival date in New Zealand and even the number of the flight and seat had to be entered here.

Less than two minutes later, the virus was back on the scene again. Two Americans arrived. They had only been in the country for a week and therefore still had to fulfil the requirement of self-isolation. They were allowed to stay at the hotel, but any contact with the staff was prohibited, so there was no room service for them.

A walk along the waterfront followed. A glass of wine in a bar that had set up sun loungers outside overlooking the water ended the day.

Virus: No, the wine doesn't conclude the day yet, I'll take care of that.

The virus determined what Sven did next. He became active on social media channels. He wrote a request to the German Foreign Office to get clarity on the rules for non-EU citizens. Let's face it, the answer came the following day by e-mail from the German Embassy in Wellington. They were asked for understanding that, due to the particular dynamics of development and the large number of requests, it could only give him general indications at present. This was followed by an invitation to register in ELEFAND and additionally on the website www.rueckholprogramm.de. Finally, a lot of links to further information were attached.

Tonight, Sven watched for the first time a press conference of Jacinda Ardern, New Zealand's Prime Minister. She impressed him. A woman who had clear goals and communicated clearly how they should be achieved. Of course, he remembered a few metrics. New Zealand reported an increase to 28 infected, the increase in Germany was more conspicuous, there were already 15,300 people infected with the virus.

Friday, March 20, 2020

Picton.

Before breakfast, Sven checked their data in the ELEFAND list and made some updates. He also wanted to register them for the return program, but the website could not be accessed.

This was not surprising, nor was the fact that the two lists had nothing to do with each other and certainly did not use a common database. On the part of the New Zealand Ministry of Health, it was once again clearly stated that all foreigners who violated the mandatory obligation of self-isolation since March 16 must leave the country immediately. Sven wrote another email, this time directly to the German embassy in Wellington, to get some assurance that Ling and he were allowed to return to Germany together.

In the somewhat run-down hotel, the rooms did not have a kitchenette. They only ate a cold breakfast. Then they made a trip to the nearby Marlborough wine-growing area, the largest on the South Island. They stopped at two wineries, but because of the harvest that had just begun, many of the trails were closed. Ling bought a beautiful Maori necklace with a green stone. In the huge plain there were numerous large wineries, whose vineyards were secured by fences because of the harvest.

Back in Picton, they went to the ferry terminal and looked at the process. In the afternoon they found a small bakery where delicious homemade cakes were baked. Customers kept their distance from each other. As a precaution, Sven had all the important documents he had taken with him printed out at the hotel. It was the residence confirmation, the letter from the Immigration Office and her marriage document. It was better to be able to show them physically if necessary.

In the evening they refueled the car, then they let themselves taste pizza and wine. People suddenly kept their distance in the restaurant, and the arrangement of the tables made it easy. Had there been any Corona-related instructions that they hadn't heard? During the daytrip, the virus was still far away, as soon as they came close to several people, it became present. This was a probably unnecessary concern, but it could no longer be suppressed.

The number of cases had risen again. On 39 in New Zealand and 19,800 in Germany. The number in New Zealand was still very low in absolute terms, but it was felt that the constant increase would have consequences. They received some good news today from the Citizen's Office of her place of residence. The eAT for Wei Ling had arrived. A member of staff sent her a photo of it, which Sven also had printed immediately. Together with the copies of the other documents, it should be possible to enter Germany without any problems. Further information received during the day was also important. New Zealand banned entry for non-New Zealanders as of now. Initial information on the return program of the Foreign Office was also available: priority would be given to travelers from "precarious" countries. There are no concrete plans for New Zealand yet. Basically, it was asked not to contact the embassy in Wellington with questions, just to wait. Impatient people were referred to further information on the website of the diplomatic mission. After the rapid changes in the last few days, the news from home remained rather barren. Sven learned that the canton of Uri in Switzerland had imposed a curfew for over-65s. Another indication that the elderly would be particularly in the spotlight in the coming measures. Otherwise, it was observed that there were now significantly more families on the field and forest roads during the week than at normal times, and all kept large distances from each other.

Saturday, March 21, 2020

Wellington. New Zealand Day 1 Corona Alert Level 2.

In the morning there was news about the return program on the Internet. 200,000 Germans would still have to be brought back, 10,000 are now being made per day. This was an impressive number, but it also made it clear that it would take a long time for the last one to be flown out. New Zealand was not yet in the return program, which meant nothing else, that at the moment no specific flight dates could be specified. Sven assumed that preparations would still be made in the background.

When they checked out, they saw a large group of Spanish travelers at the reception.

Virus: Spaniards! Risk!

They waited for a gap, returned the room key and quickly disappeared. They parked the rental car in the Hertz parking lot, and handed over the vehicle key to the employee in the barracks nearby.

They were early on and were among the first to check in at the ferry terminal. A leash had been stretched in front of the counter where the boarding passes were issued. "Please keep a distance of 2 meters," was said on a sign. On the ferry were mainly railway wagons and trucks, along with some buses. The number of foot passengers was certainly less than 60 and spread loosely over numerous decks. More distance was not possible. The ride began at 10:50 a.m. For 90 minutes they sailed over mirror-smooth water through fjord-like sea arms overlooking a pure world of rolling hills, coves and a few tiny fishing villages. Even for the remaining 90 minutes over the open Cook Strait, the sea remained fairly calm. They sat on the top deck most of the time despite the cool wind. Barely six other people could stand it here. The pure sea air was absolutely Corona free.

Virus: The gentleman in the back, who coughs constantly, may be infected by me.

Sven: Why? Just because he speaks Swiss German?

Virus: Did you forget that I was already with you in Zurich?

In Wellington, they had to wait to get out because the pedestrian terminal could not be used for repair work. The staff handed out sweet candy from a basket. Then a double-decker bus on level 4, the car deck, stood ready and brought them ashore. The suitcases were already rolling on the output belt and they were also able to take over the new rental car quickly. Another Toyota Corolla, this time in silver grey.

The drive to the hotel, which was close to the city center, led via numerous detours because of the construction sites across the city, which was laid out on countless hills. The hotel had a dungeon-like underground car park and the room was small and uncomfortable. When checking in, the first thing the virus asked through the staff member's mouth at the front desk was if they wanted to leave? It looked like a hammer blow. For the first time, Corona became a palpable threat.

The sky was covered and it started to drizzle. Nevertheless, they explored the city center and the riverside promenade. Nothing was appealing, an unsightly architecture. The occasional colonial buildings that catch the eye turned out to be a forgery. Only the facade had been designed accordingly. There were some cool skateboarders at the Warf, there were some expensive restaurants. They chose a fish restaurant.

Before ordering, the virus put a list on the table: Please enter both names, e-mail and address here.

The waiter made sure that the few guests used tables far apart from each other.

A total of 52 cases were reported in New Zealand today. When they returned to the hotel, they were informed that the government had declared Alert Level 2 (out of 4). Sven searched the Internet for more background and found the following definition for Alert Level 2:

„Where the disease is contained, but the risks are growing because we have more cases. This is when we move to reduce our contact with one another, we increase our border measures and we cancel events. This is also the level where we ask people to work differently if they can, and cancel unnecessary travel.“

He was impressed by the way in which this crisis and the measures needed to combat. It was described so clearly and systematically. How much more complicated and confused would this be in Germany at the moment?

For the two of them, an arrangement in it was particularly important: reduce non required travel! Holiday trips should therefore also be reduced. The New Zealand government, according to Sven's interpretation, did not wait for stricter measures until the child had fallen into the well. From the very first infected, the health department analyzed the origin of the cases very meticulously. All 52 had a travel background and had introduced the virus from abroad. The government had already set up a Corona website where Sven found the recording of the press conference with Jacinda Ardern. In clear terms, she gave very precise reasons for the decision to impose initial restrictions already now. New Zealand is a small country, she said, so absolute case numbers must always be put in relation to the total population. That, as everyone knows, is less than 5 million. Then came her decisive sentence: "Italy had only 100 cases not long ago." She didn't have to say more. Journalists had many questions, but no one criticized the decision.

Sven cancelled the second night in Wellington. The hotel management had full understanding of this and waived the cancellation fee normally due. They would head to the middle of the North Island tomorrow so they could be at Auckland Airport at any time in a day. They knew that Alert Level 2 would not be the highest level.

Sunday, March 22, 2020

Taupo. New Zealand Day 2 Corona Alert Level 2.

They took a standard breakfast at the hotel, then Sven took the car out of the dimly underground car park and carefully steered it outside through a pile of rubble. Soon they were on

Highway Number 1 northbound. After half an hour, the foothills of Wellington were just behind them, the route guidance system played a confusing game with them. The huge construction sites on the motorway were unknown to him, again and again it wanted to lead them on roads and exits that did not exist. After asking for advice at a gas station and with a local in a side street, they were finally back on track. It was hilly and the road stretched out along the sea for a while. Mostly it rained. Later, as the rain subsided, they stopped at some vantage points. In the small town of Taihape they bought something, later in Taupo they supplemented their stock.

In the early afternoon they were welcomed by the friendly owner of the motel in Taupo. They had ripped her off the sofa and interrupted her Netflix series. Apart from them, only one other couple would stay here today, the woman said. The small apartment in the motel was beautifully located, well furnished, lightning-clean and had a whirlpool. From the terrace they saw the Lake Taupo just 100 meters away, over whose water still heavy grey clouds hung. Only the fridge had a small shortcoming. The bottle holder on the inside door was mounted far too low. When Sven opened it with momentum, the bottle of Chardonnay, intended for the evening, flew out onto the tiled floor and all the beautiful contents flowed into the carpet and poured over the stones. Well, the supermarket wasn't far away, he quickly drove back while Ling was preparing dinner, and bought a new bottle. They ate fish and slowly became worried about the way forward.

Virus, quite constructive: You should think carefully about what you are doing next.

Sven almost did not take note of the figures from China, which reported more and more healed and hardly any new infections, which had no meaning for him at the moment. For Ling, however, it was important. Joy and pride were not to be overlooked. Sven had been studying the values from Europe, especially Italy, Spain and the head-to-head race between

France and Germany for days, but he read only superficially about the measures already decided or planned there. That was so far away at the moment. Early enough, they would be confronted with it.

In the evening, the quirky but very noble lady of the house knocked on the door to offer to stay as long as they wanted for a special price. She would close all other facilities and rooms of her motel the day after tomorrow. Tomorrow there would be an important announcement from the government, but she already knew that her business with tourists would come to a standstill for a long period. They would consider it and thanked warmly for the kindly offer, was Sven's answer.

The embassy in Wellington informed on its website that registration for the return program could now be made, because a new program had been made available with the help of SAP within a very short time. Well then, thought Sven after the meal, I will register. In fact, the program was opened easily and he entered his data. Name, date of birth, passport number, country of stay, preferred airport of departure and arrival. A little bit of data for a machine-based planning of the return action, he thought. Well, yes. In another part there were data fields for fellow passengers. He entered Ling's name, date of birth and passport number. There was no more available. He used an additional text box to enter their current whereabouts. That was certainly useful information for the planning team, he thought. After sending the data, he waited for confirmation by e-mail, which did not arrive. So then just look at the data again, his brain controlled it. But that was not possible. Did the virus also infect the team of programmers? Because he was unsure, but definitely wanted to be registered in the return program, he started from scratch, with the same result. After a third attempt, he gave up for today. He later learned that many other desperate people had entered their data several times, some a dozen times. All for the same reason. He knew the problem and already knew that the embassy with the data would certainly not have an easy job. Later in the evening, news arrived that Emirates would suspend all flights worldwide from March 25. This left many people stranded in New Zealand, as Emirates was one of the most used airlines to come here from Europe.

Rather incidentally, the observation was that the daily values of the RKI and the JHU again showed significant deviations from each other. Well, for the European countries, this was no longer really important because of the high number and New Zealand had no differences. The local authorities had no problem reporting accurate, consistent figures once a day. There had already been 102, while Germany counted nearly 25,000 infected.

Monday, March 23, 2020

Napier. New Zealand Day 1 Corona Alert Level 3.

That night, they had thought about the way they went on their journey. They wanted to use the few days of free travel to see at least part of the North Island. That's why they turned down the nice lady's offer and set off. Their current destination was Napier on the east coast.

The lockdown was imminent, she told them. Important decisions would be communicated during the day. You should therefore take a look at the government's website more often.

After breakfast, they walked along the shore path of Lake Taupo. It was still raining a little bit, but they wanted to see something from the place. They walked past the Yacht Club, then through Riverside Park. They continued to the Craters of the Moon. When they arrived, it was just five kilometers from the town center, even a bit of sun came through the clouds. For a small entrance fee, they went on the one-hour round-the-post without knowing exactly what to expect. The surprise was all the greater. They walked through a truly alien landscape, over which the swathes of gas mist swelled from dozens of holes in the ground. In some places it stank for sulfur. The mud holes were particularly impressive. They bubbled loudly and the leakage of the gases produced an eerie hissing. Maybe ten more visitors were on the way here, at normal times there would be hundreds.

They went on to the nearby Huka Falls. Through a narrow gorge the river roared, in order to shoot out at the end not very deep but with enormous thunder and passed into a wide river course. The parking lot was already closed, but the car was still allowed to park on the road. A handful of people also watched the spectacle.

Then they were on the road to Napier on the Pacific Coast. First, they went through an almost endless plateau, where huge amounts of trees had been felled. Gentle-green hill country followed, finally moving into a fruit and wine-growing area in the plain. They refueled the car and reached a beautiful large motel, right on the waterfront, with a spacious balcony facing the sea. They had arrived at a ghostly-looking place. Only three other cars were parked in the parking lot. At the reception, they were informed without emotion that the motel would close the day after tomorrow, as were all the other places in the village. There were two reasons why the motels ceased operations, Sven learned from the employee. No more customers, be the one, the fear of the staff of being infected by the virus the other. An American couple arrived. They had booked a room through Airbnb, but were kicked out by the owner who closed his house today. They were helpless as to how to proceed. A New Zealand pensioner couple was better off. They had already completed their journey and wanted to go to Wellington tomorrow in their rental car and fly from there to Christchurch, where they lived. A day before the lockdown, they would be home.

Prime Minister Ardern had announced the decisions in the afternoon. New Zealand have been at Alert Level 3 since today, with Alert Level 4 set to take place from Wednesday

23:59. At the same time, a national emergency was declared. Sven found the definition of Level 3 on the website:

„Alert Level three is where the disease is increasingly difficult to contain. This is where we restrict our contact by stepping things up again. We close public venues and ask non-essential businesses to close."

Decisions were taken quickly. All travelers, locals, businessmen, in short, all those who were in the country, had just over 48 hours to prepare for it. For Sven and Ling, this meant: End of the journey! No more sightseeing, no exploring new places and areas, no more restaurants, virtually a curfew, except grocery shopping and short walks. They decided to move into a motel with a kitchen near Auckland Airport from Wednesday, stock up on food and wait for things there.

Nevertheless, they enjoyed coffee and cake on the balcony and took a long walk on the black Pacific beach. A few joggers and cyclists were on the way, along with a few people with their camper van, who had set up their tables outside and cooked. Otherwise it was already empty in Napier. Two days later, all had to return their vans because the places with electricity and water connection were also closed.

In the late afternoon they drove to the supermarket and met for the first time a long queue of waiting people. Today there was a kind of heaviness over the country, the laughter had disappeared, already there was single entry, monitored by security personnel. A local with large gaps in her teeth told them that she had to endure for more than an hour until she was allowed in. Sven and Ling had time, waited and bought food and drinks for the next three days. In the super market, they felt a fictitious threat. They hustled from one row of shelves to the next, only to be quickly out again. Totally irrational, but what was now still under control of the mind?

In the evening it was still warm enough to eat on the balcony.

Virus: Today, Etihad has also completely suspended operations and Singapore has closed its airport.

Anti-virus: They booked their return flight with Qatar Airways.

Virus: Transit in Bangkok is now only allowed for those who can provide a current health certificate including a negative Corona test.

Anti-virus: Doha is still open for normal transit.

Sven informed family and friends about the current situation. He wrote to them that from Thursday the police and military would oversee the curfew, describing the Prime Minister as a strong figure who had a clear plan and was 100 percent supported by her ministers and advisers. Mrs. Ardern had not yet said anything about the situation for tourists, who generate a large part of New Zealand's prosperity.

In the evening, Sven called Qatar Airways again to ask for the possibility of an earlier return flight. There was one, on April 29, but at an extra cost of 3,000 euros per person. He left everything to the old. It was too early to make panicky decisions.

The figures tonight was completely incidental. 102 infected in New Zealand, 29,100 in Germany. Sven and Ling were satisfied with their plan under the new situation. They would act in accordance with the conditions and then simply wait and see what happens.

Tuesday, March 24, 2020

Rotorua. New Zealand Day 2 Corona Alert Level 3.

Their sleep was restless. They had booked a motel in Rotorua for the next night, because they wanted to drive a large part of the route to Auckland already today. They set off at 9 o'clock, after breakfast on the balcony, a few hundred meters towards the city center. There they parked their car in a parking lot with a parking meter, for which no one showed any more interest. They walked through three streets of the beautiful Art Deco district, the new downtown. A sign with the simple inscription "Closed" was glued to almost all shops. The lockdown requirements were implemented two days before it came into force. A few pedestrians got lost in the otherwise bustling streets. Today, the city center was orphaned. There was silence. In the shop of a large gas station they wanted to buy some groceries, but it was already closed. You could still refuel, whereby payment was only possible at a small window. No one was allowed to enter the interior.

The journey went back to Taupo, where they arrived at 12 o'clock. They quickly shopped in the local supermarket because they knew which things were on which shelves. Also, a large bag of rice, a bottle of soya and Chinese spices, stock for several days. The weather was quite nice, so they took time for a walk along Lake Taupo. Then they drove without any further stop to Rotorua. Their motel was still open today. It was empty. Only one other couple had booked here for one night. The friendly woman at the reception could not say what the situation would be tomorrow in the airport hotels and motels. She seemed depressed because she would have no revenue in the next few weeks, no earnings for at least a month.

Prime Minister Ardern explained in the afternoon the measures, which would come into force from Thursday, gave clear instructions and was clear with what she expected from her compatriots.

»Stay home, be kind, break the chain of transmission«. Simple, clear, unambiguous.

The number of people infected was 155, most of whom had imported the virus from abroad. But there have also been the first cases of infection within the New Zealand society. The number in Germany had risen to 33,300.

Sven and Ling took a walk to the city center. In the middle of it was a large area from which it smoldered, stank and bubbled. Mystical plumes of fog lay over the former crater. Was no one worried that these volcanic gases would explode and destroy the whole city one day? The place was one of the magnets for tourists. Today they were the only ones strolling around. The Maori Village, a well-known open-air museum, was already closed, but you could still roam the outdoor facilities. Particularly impressive were the large white tombs, which protruded one meter above the ground. The promenade along the lake was deserted. Only in the park in front of the beautifully half-timbered city museum a few people walked around, no more than ten. A three-meter high fence had been erected in front of the museum. The signs read "Closed". English-maintained lawns, majestic trees and many flowers told of a healed world. On the way back they passed two big hotels, Pullmann and Ibis. Both had already ceased operations. A few buses were waiting at the stops. The drivers sat lonely in their seats, passengers could not be seen far and wide. Ling and Sven found a bit of relaxation in the motel's large pool, which was filled with hot thermal water. They then roasted fish and ate potatoes with vegetables.

Virus: You will sleep restlessly, Sven Neuland. It came as punctually as the sandman from childhood.

Sven: This is not new for me.

Virus: You need to read the latest news.

Sven found an e-mail from the German Foreign Office: "We have found that unfortunately you have entered in at least one entry in the program "Germany", "Alemania" or "Allemagne" as your current place of residence. Instead, we need unconditionally the name of the country where you currently are, which you best choose exclusively from the dropdown menu and do not enter your own text". As strange as this message was, it proved that the data had arrived in the return app. And behold, suddenly the contents were also visible and also changeable. Sven checked the entry in the country of residence field. New Zealand was there. What had the

Foreign Office seen? In a text box, he updated their whereabouts: Rotorua.

He called the Phoenix video library following a friend's advice. There, Foreign Minister Heiko Maas announced that there would soon be also return flights from New Zealand. That made them optimistic. However, no new information has been received from the embassy for two days. Meanwhile, there was a Facebook group of the stranded Germans. This quickly became the central source of information.

Sven checked the booking of the motel near Auckland Airport. He had initially reserved for five days. The booking was still confirmed, but he still slept restlessly. How much the confirmation was worth, they would know in twelve hours.

Wednesday, March 25, 2020

Auckland. New Zealand Day 3 Corona Alert Level 3.

Ling was, as always, quite calm, but Sven was restless, he wanted to arrive in Auckland early. If their motel was to be closed, he wanted to have enough time to find an alternative. That's why they had a quick breakfast at 7:30 a.m. Their neighbors, the only other guests at the motel, which closed for at least four weeks today, left at 8 a.m. They were New Zealanders and had to travel to the south of the North Island to be home on time for the lockdown. At 8:30 a.m., Sven and Ling set off. Car traffic was still normal, but the large 8-lane expressway connecting Hamilton to Auckland was already very empty. At the slopes, he overtook ten other cars today, more than in the whole of three weeks before. Today there was no time for leisure at the wheel and stops on the way.

Virus: Do you think the motel is open?
Sven: We'll see, I don't know.
Ling: Nonsense, of course it will be open.

Virus: Maybe not.

Anti-virus: Many people will drive near the airport. The hotels have to stay open. Where are people supposed to stay?

Again, and again while driving, the virus controlled his thoughts. Today already in the early morning. That was not new. The Best Western Motel was easy to find. Arriving at 11:20 a.m., they rushed to the reception.

"Yes, we will remain open all the time during the lockdown, don't worry."

The Indian staff was totally relaxed. Great relief at Sven. It was the expected statement, Ling found. They would have a roof over their heads at the time of the lockdown. That was the most important thing.

They familiarized themselves with the area via Google Maps and Baidu Maps. A large supermarket was only 1.5 kilometers away. Everything done right.

They should wait 90 minutes, then they could already go to the room, to their home for the next 3, 7, 12, or whatever days. Ling and Sven set off for a walk to a nature reserve. It lasted two hours. There were some of them nearby, which would make the isolation more bearable, because walks in the fresh air were still allowed. The only thing that was not forbidden besides shopping for food, provided you stayed in your "bubble". Several other foreigners were also seen in the area. There were people with the same destiny, there were many of them. Germans, British, Americans, Spaniards.

Then they moved into their studio. It had a bedroom, a living room with kitchen and another bed, and a bathroom with hot tub. They were on the first floor, where there were ten apartments. There was a veranda overlooking the courtyard and the smaller building opposite.

At 2 p.m. they drove to the supermarket. It was one from the well-known PAK'nSAVE chain. They bought food for two days and refueled the car. People were already waiting in queues outside, only a certain number of shoppers were allowed to stay in the store at the same time. The discipline of those waiting was exemplary. People with masks were very numerous. Ling also pulled over one, Sven was still hesitant today, he wanted to keep his masks for Germany. There he would rather need them. He remained cautious, because buying face masks in Germany was not possible at the moment. They bought four glasses of Manuka-honey, which would be their souvenir, along with beef, potatoes, vegetables, wine, fruit, rolls, sausage, cheese, butter, tomatoes and cakes. They didn't want to go to the supermarket every day, but they didn't want to shop too much if they could fly back at short notice. It was difficult to find a balance. Back at the motel, it was time to relax. The WI-FI was extremely slow. Why just now that you really needed it? Ling bought Chinese WI-FI for three days. It was as fast as you'd expect. Sven had no idea how it worked technically, nor did Ling, but that was insignificant.

6:30 p.m.: Alarm on any mobile phone! A text was sent and read at the same time:

NATIONAL EMERGENCY MANAGEMENT AGENCY ALERT: From 11:59pm tonight, the whole of New Zealand moves to COVID-19 Alert Level 4.

This message is for all of New Zealand. We are depending on you.

Follow the rules and STAY HOME. Act as if you have COVID-19. This will save lives.

Remember:

Where you stay tonight is where YOU MUST stay from now on.

You must only be in physical contact with those you are living with.

It is likely Level 4 measures will stay in place for a number of weeks.

Let's all do our bit to unite against COVID-19.

Kia kaha.

Issued 25 March 2020 6:30pm.

There are 6 1/2 hours left until the lockdown. There were special programs on television, Countdown to Lockdown. New Zealand came to a standstill. All behavioral measures have been explained. It was about the "bubble", the small circle of people in which one had to spend the next four weeks. A "bubble" could be an individual, a couple or a family. Nobody was allowed to switch from his "bubble" to another during the next four weeks and no one was allowed to let others into his own "bubble". It was good to consider who you would be with at midnight today. You were allowed to talk to people from another "bubble" if you kept at least 2 meters distance.

The beef tasted very good. Ling had put it in soya and honey.

At midnight today, there were 205 people infected in New Zealand. With this value began the long way to eliminate the transmission of the virus within New Zealand society started. That was the goal. At 11:59 p.m., the national state of emergency came into effect, Alert Level 4, just three days after Alert Level 3! Without compromise.

"We have to!" said the Prime Minister.

Today, the figures from other countries, including those from Germany, were meaningless. In the evening Sven informed the people at home about their personal situation and the political decisions.

Sven: Everything except grocery stores, pharmacy and some petrol stations is closed.

Family: How about bakeries, butchers, restaurants?

Sven: All closed. Manufacturing is completely suspended, wherever possible, must be worked from home. The entire medical service continues as before, schools, university services and all leisure facilities are closed, culture and sporting events are cancelled. The opening hours in the super market have been shortened, there is a maximum amount of people who are allowed into the store. Long queues of waiting people outside. Everything is strictly controlled.

A friend was sure that such rigorous measures cannot be sustained for long. Would he be right?

Lockdown – In New Zealand

Thursday, March 26, 2020

Auckland. New Zealand Day 1 Corona Alert Level 4.

Again, Sven woke up twice in the night. Each time he reached for his mobile phone. In the morning, an email arrived from New Zealand Immigration. They were informed that all visas had been automatically renewed until the end of September 2020. That was, after all, positive news in the event of a case. Then he re-studied the definition of Alert Level 4:

„This is where we have sustained transmission. This is where we eliminate contact with each other altogether. We keep essential services going, but we ask everyone to stay at home until COVID-19 is back under control. We have to focus on one simple goal – to slow down COVID-19. Slowing it down, means not having one big tidal wave of cases, but instead, smaller waves – groups of cases that we can manage properly as they arise. That means we reduce the impact on health, on jobs and on our economy. Some countries have successfully managed to do this – but it does mean we have to be ready to step up our action when we need to. The alert system will apply to the whole country for now, but as the pandemic continues levels may only apply to certain New Zealand towns or cities."

In the morning they took a walk north. They started at the motel; the car remained in the parking lot. They behaved in an exemplary manner. Here was a residential area where rather poor people seemed to live, many Maori among them. Along the way, they passed huge cemeteries and tombs, where even the national flags of the deceased were attached. In front of a grave, three young Maori men sat in grass. Probably one of her relatives had recently died. They seemed lost in their minds.

Ling urged Sven to return the rental car. It didn't make sense to keep it longer because they weren't allowed to use it anyway. Earlier returns may have resulted in a refund of unused days. At the reception, Sven was informed that it was not a problem to go to the rental car return at the airport, only the terminal itself was closed. They were also offered to be picked up by the motel shuttle bus. There were no police on the four kilometers, there were no barriers or controls. They parked the car in the car park, in the Hertz row. A counter window was open at the exit. They returned the key and the worker told them that the unused days would definitely be refunded. They decided to walk back to the motel and strolled five kilometers along logistics centers, freight forwarders and large motorhome parking lots. All places were full, all campers had been given back. One could guess what loss of revenue this meant for the landlords. Along the way, they met a few other foreigners. Everyone was waiting, no one would walk through this area at normal times. Coffee and cakes on the terrace followed, in the evening again beef, vegetables and potatoes. This time they had put the meat heavily in Manuka-honey, which gave it an excellent taste. It was followed by a conversation with a young Spanish couple who lived two rooms away. It was on honeymoon. They were originally scheduled to fly back on April 1, but Qatar Airways had cancelled that flight. After all, they were rebooked to April 4. So, they had a perspective. They would fly via London to Madrid and hoped that transit in Great Britain would be easy. Above all, however, they expected Qatar Airways to maintain operations. Sven and Ling also wanted this. There were still a few cars driving through the area, but New Zealanders could hardly be seen on the road.

In their motel, the stranded got to know each other superficially. They talked to each other about the situation and who had received what information. This were brief conversations and everyone hoped to be at the first to be brought back.

Today there was new information from the embassy. On Facebook, not by e-mail. It said the government had reached an agreement with Air New Zealand to help with the return flights. The first two flights were scheduled to depart on Saturday. You will be informed a few hours before departure. That was good news. However, 12,000 people wanted going home, that would take more than two weeks. The embassy decides who is allowed to fly on which day.

Sven: Let's see when we're at it?

Ling: I think very soon. We are already at the airport.

On the first day of the lockdown, New Zealand had 283 infected. Of course, the numbers would go up further at first. It would take two weeks to determine whether the measures were successful.

After the meal there was time for the daily Corona update. Read and send information. Today came a response from the BMI, the Federal Ministry of the Interior. Sven had also asked about the entry regulations here, and this ministry was responsible for this. Again, he did not receive a specific answer, instead he was referred to the websites of the Federal Police. The latter is ultimately responsible for who they reject at the border.

There was confusion about the entry of fellow passengers in the return app. The embassy said that companions should not be registered separately, a consulate general said the opposite. What did they do in this case? Sven opted for double registration and explained the interdependence in the text field. Even when he wrote, he knew that he would not make planning easier.

The news from Germany included the following information:

A discussion had already begun on how to get out of the strict regulation of social contacts and the closure of shops.

Sweden was chosen by the opponents of the German measures as an example of a different approach. There, almost nothing was restricted and it seemed to be crowned with success.

In German hospitals, to the surprise of many, enough beds are available. For this reason, French intensive patients would also be treated in Germany.

Sven learned that from Saturday in New Zealand all domestic flights would also be cancelled. Only those working for essential services were allowed to use planes. This would become a problem for those who have not been close to the airport.

In the evening they sat with a glass of wine at the door on the porch, everyone else had already retreated to their rooms. Sven wanted to know how his friends' lives had already changed. One who otherwise took little part in the WhatsApp chats was very happy to write: "I already feel the limitations. No university, no swimming, no tennis, no Pilates, no conviviality, no eating with the tennis group. At the moment, this is not a problem. I watch TV, stream on Netflix, read, play a lot of chess against the computer, eat with the family, jog and ride a bike. But in the long run it will be annoying. I suspect that the restrictions will apply to us older people for a year. If the number of cases subsides, schools, universities, etc. will reopen, transport and economic life will be facilitated. This will lead to a further increase in the number of cases and a further tightening of the restrictions. It's not gone until there's a vaccine. I also miss the Bundesliga and the Champions League".

Flightradar24 has now become an app that Sven regularly used to inform himself about arriving and departing aircraft, because the embassy learned little about it. He saw that a Lufthansa B747 had landed in Auckland and was due to fly back at 9am tomorrow morning. It became real. Who would get seats in this machine?

Friday, March 27, 2020

Auckland. New Zealand Day 2 Corona Alert Level 4.

That night Sven finally slept through again. It was already eight o'clock when he woke up. They had already become accustomed to their lockdown. It was too early to worry; they got used to their new everyday life. This was not difficult, because the barriers were so strict that it made no sense to think about variants of the design. In the morning he searched for news on WhatsApp, Facebook and the embassy's website. There was no. It was raining, but some other waiting people had already opened the doors and leaned on the railing of the porch, looking for fellow sufferers, for conversation partners. The first return flight with the Lufthansa aircraft, announced for today, did not take place, it had been postponed by one day to Saturday morning.

In fact, some people had already received an email from the embassy that they had a seat on the first plane. You should arrive at the airport by 6 a.m. at the latest. Others had an email in their inbox saying they were on a reserve list. They were also asked to go to the airport. In case not all passengers had arrived at 6 a.m., they would get a seat, at least some of them. On the part of the embassy, there was no information on the criteria for the selection, including no information on the next flights. Sven hoped that real hardship cases, young people travelling alone, the sick, parents with infants would be allowed to fly first.

Every afternoon there were now two press conferences. In the first, at 1 p.m., very detailed was reported on the number of infected, their origin, reason of infection, deaths, number of tests and recoveries. That was the part of Dr. Ashley Bloomfield, Director-General of Health. Two to three times a week he was represented by Dr. Caroline McElnay, Director of Public Health. The press conference at 3 p.m. was about the program as a whole. That was the job of Prime Minister Jacinda Ardern, who was represented by Hon Grant Robertson, the Minister for the Finance. These events lasted between 40 and 50 minutes. They gave journalists ample opportunity to ask their questions. From now on Sven saw one every day, when the time also adapted both press conferences. On the one hand, he gained interesting information, and on the other hand, they were an impressive example of how such events can be made rich in content, an example of great communication. He did not know this from his home experience. Today, Mrs. Ardern had an important message: Many Germans who are to be brought back to Germany via the Federal Government's return program are not near Auckland or Christchurch airports. It lacks a strategy on the part of the federal government on how these people can get to one of the airports without endangering the health of even one New Zealander. She would allow time until March 31 to present this strategy. Until then, there will be no return flights. That was a deep hit. The flight planned for Saturday was nevertheless allowed to take off because she granted an exemption.

Sven and Ling took a short walk to the small airport supermarket, just 300 meters away. A few people waited in a queue and kept enough distance. Only one person was allowed into the store at a time, in total there were no more than five people in at a time. The offer was small and not very appealing. They only bought a few cans, ice cream and biscuits. A mobile test station had been set up next to the supermarket, but only few could be seen which have just been tested. Then they went the slightly longer way, which took twenty minutes, to PAK'nSAVE. A few foreigners were, by a large distance to each other, also on the way to that location. In front of the entrance, people waited in a long, quiet, very disciplined queue. All kept enough distance from each other. Their waiting time was about 30 minutes, but that didn't matter, because they had enough time. The shelves were well filled. They got everything they were looking for: meat, wine, rolls, pastries, vegetables, fruit, water. It would be enough for three days. Everywhere, especially in front of the checkout area, "keep 2-meters distance" signs had been glued to the floor and to the walls. At the checkout, the handles of the shopping carts and the keyboards for PIN entry were sterilized after each customer. They took it very seriously. Afterwards there was coffee and cake on the terrace, reading, Facebook search. After dinner, they took a short walk around the block. An everyday routine had already developed. When they returned, a group of Germans stood in the parking lot. Short discussions were held on the provisional halt to the return flight operation. Everyone was disappointed, angry, but still optimistic. It was known that all would stay here together for at least the next five days. The Bavarian couple, who planned to shorten the waiting time by short trips by car, had also returned their Alamo rental car. They, too, were too likely to be caught. On Facebook, there were first desperate messages about the delay. Some parents were very worried because their minor children wanted to return alone, but were still somewhere inland, far from the airport. This was all the worse because the last regular domestic flights were cancelled from midnight.

Sven took a look at the Qatar Airways website. He called the status page. Their flight on April 7 was still confirmed. But as soon as they got seats on one of the return planes, they would take them and cancel their regular ticket. This was possible free of charge up to three days before departure. It was still long until April 7. The flight was eventually cancelled at any time.

He read the numbers of those infected in Germany and elsewhere in Europe from the display of the mobile phone and had forgotten them a minute later. In New Zealand, 368 people were now reported as infected, a significant increase. He remembered that number. He understood now why recently some people in the motels and shops said that the lockdown in New Zealand had come too late. Decided too late, just having 75 cases? How many cases had there been in Germany when the rip line was pulled there? One of the friends in Germany, however, judged the whole action in New Zealand as a panic reaction that was not appropriate to the real threat. Who could say which strategy was the right one?

Saturday, March 28, 2020

Auckland. New Zealand Day 3 Corona Alert Level 4.

Sven woke up after having a good night's rest around 8:30 a.m. Outside was clear blue sky, the air was still fresh, about 10 degrees. Breakfast in their new home had already become a standardized process. Coffee, soft sesame bread, topped with pastrami, with some Gouda cheese with garlic, a tomato, eggs, orange juice. The New Zealand orange juice tasted fresh and fruity. Ling drank milk every morning. She was very enthusiastic about the taste. Much more substantial than in Germany and anyway by lengths better than the aqueous milk in China.

Today they didn't have to go to the supermarket. After breakfast, they set off for a three-hour hike west to the Otuataua Stonefields Historic Reserve. There were still cars on the road, hard to tell if they were all essential services. A few cyclists kept fit, but there were never more than two together.

They met a few tourists in the waiting area, who also went for a walk here. They, too, complied with the rules and were only travelling in pairs. It was quiet, so that the take-off of a plane from the airport next door could be clearly heard. Then they could see the machine. It was Lufthansa's B747 clearly visible on the rear wing. The first 400 people were on their way via Tokyo to Frankfurt.

Sven: When do you think it's our turn?

Ling: It won't take more than a few days.

Virus: Keep on dreaming.

The shallow bay where the Historic Reserve was located had only a narrow strait connecting to the open sea. Hundreds of birds stalked through the mud in search of edibles. Small trees, which temporarily became aquatic plants with the approaching tide, stood close to the shore.

At 2 p.m. they were back, time to rest, read, write. The Englishman, who arrived yesterday and wanted to fly to London today via Hong Kong, was still there. He was not allowed to check in because he was not allowed to transit in Hong Kong. Nevertheless, he remained optimistic and took phone calls for a long time to research new flight options. The New Zealander, who had an American green card, was still hoping to fly to Los Angeles tomorrow.

At the motel it was quiet. The two young women, who lived opposite the house, lay as always in the grass next to the parking lots. One read, the other spent ten hours a day on her mobile phone. Other waiting people sat in their chair in front of their room for a while. The embassy posted on its website yesterday's decision of the New Zealand government. Of course, everyone already knew.

Sven posted a few photos of today's walk in the Facebook group and encouraged the other waiting people to go outside as well. The reactions arrived in minutes. Some liked the suggestion, others were shocked because they thought Sven was calling for a bigger day trip and was blatantly and consciously violating the "Stay Home" obligation, to the detriment of all those stranded.

A woman, around fifty, from northern Germany had kept her rental car. She drove through the area until she was stopped by police. She knew that the first offence would only be punished with a friendly admonition.

In today's press conference, details of the development of the last twenty-four hours were announced. More than 451 New Zealanders were reported infected, the vast majority of whom had a travel history, i.e. the virus imported from abroad. Behavioral measures such as washing hands and so on were repeated prayerfully. On TV, corresponding spots ran, at least once per hour.

A logo has been created. All COVID-19 messages were on a yellow-and-white hatched background. It was released for private use. On the website of the Ministry of Health, a list was kept from the first infected person, in which each case was documented. Among the items included their place of residence, age group, flight number, test date and further information. This list has also been continued as the numbers continue to grow.

German media also wrote of the temporary failure of the return program from New Zealand.

Sven booked more days at the motel. The Qatar Airways flight was still reported as confirmed. Around 5 p.m., the news circulated that new data fields had now been added to the registration program. The information came from a user from the Facebook group, not the embassy. Sven would try it tomorrow. Facebook also posted photos of lucky ones getting a seat on the first flight this morning. They showed the long queue at check-in and cheerful faces.

Sunday, March 29, 2020

Auckland. New Zealand Day 4 Corona Alert Level 4.

The motel management had arranged that no one who had made another booking had to change the room. It was very pleasant. Many had made a kind of friendship with the cleaning staff. All those who lived, waited or worked here had already become a large family.

The Englishman next door hoped to come to London tonight via San Francisco and Dallas. He had been told that transit was possible for him in the United States. Sven gave him a thumbs up.

Sven and Ling wanted to buy masks at the nearby pharmacy, but the store was closed today, it was Sunday. In the small supermarket next door, it was very empty. They bought coke, water and ice. The refreshing taste of the ice-cold Coke was one of the few variations in the daily monotony.

At noon they set off for their daily walk. For nearly three hours, they explored the south side of Puketutu Island. Initially, they were travelling alone, but by the early afternoon a number of other groups of 2 or 3 people had come here to get their legs off.

At coffee time there was ice cream and cake, then Sven followed Jacinda Ardern's daily press conference. The government today issued a formal specification for "Local Walks". They are walks that start at the apartment and each of which can return home at any time without the help of others. Now they knew. The Prime Minister went on to say that a further increase in the number of people infected was to be expected for a few more days. It is only in a week's time that the first findings can be drawn as to whether the lockdown worked. Now 514 people are infected, most of them new infected are still from abroad. Her comments on inpatient treatment were also noteworthy: hospitals had sent home all patients whose treatment was not urgently needed. As a result, normal utilization was reduced from 90% to 50% in order to provide free places for those suffering from Corona. She also set up a website to report anyone who observed people or companies who did not comply with the lockdown requirements. Denunciation would probably be called this with us, Sven thought. There was no news about the return program and the embassy was silent.

Sven and Ling rested with the room door open, it started to rain slightly. Apart from the two girls in the house opposite, no one was sitting on the porch. The washing machine, which has been running almost continuously over the past few days, also remained calm today.

In the Facebook group there was again a lot of discussion about whether couples should register individually or register each other as fellow travelers. Another topic was whether you should delete your own data if you had registered several times. Many had a great interest in precise data. No one knew a workable solution, because there was no function for deleting fellow passengers or for entire registrations. Sven called up their registration data and found the fields that had become new in flight. He filled them out: the place and date of issue of the passport, the exact place of residence in Germany. But the fields so important for the planning were still missing about the exact location in New Zealand. Many people were worried by now that for this reason it would be nothing with the hoped-for return flight. Everything didn't seem professional. The Qatar Airways website also said today that their flight was still confirmed. They counted the days. At worst, ten more. But if they soon got a return flight, which they would take of course, it would be significantly less.

At night, a long report of a woman sitting on the first return plane caused a stir. She wrote that the night before the flight, she called the embassy directly to ask if she could fly with it. Shortly afterwards, she received an e-mail with the flight confirmation. The embassy had always clearly urged people to refrain from making calls because no one could actively claim a seat anyway. Obviously, it worked. Outrage among young parents waiting here with babies, outrage among sick people who needed medication. This was followed by a description of the flight. What could you expect? They were brought home. What was the service? Not even that of a normal flight in economy class. The check-in was extremely lengthy and the boarding passes were issued manually.

At the end of the day, Sven looked at Europe's statistics. Germany had 62,400 cases. That was dramatic when you put it in relation to the beginning of March. Those who wanted to gloss over the situation simply took countries that were even worse off. Over 80,000 in Spain, 102,000 in Italy, 162,000 in the US. Germany could have been compared to other countries, but it did not do so because the government wanted to send out the signal that it had everything under control.

In Germany, daylight saving time had come into force, reducing the time difference to eleven hours.

Sven in a WhatsApp message: We have already come an hour closer today.

Friend-1: There seems to be a change of mind when it comes to wearing masks. A month ago, they were described as completely pointless, and even harmful. Now individual companies are starting to import masks in large numbers from China. The Ministry of Health had significantly eased the tendering rules for the purchase of masks.

Friend -2: Not only that, more and more companies in Germany are now starting to make masks themselves.

Sven: Then the bottleneck in the pharmacies will soon be eliminated.

Friend-2: Of course not, because these masks are made of simple cotton fabrics. They are not surgical masks.

Monday, March 30, 2020

Auckland. New Zealand Day 5 Corona Alert Level 4.

The embassy asked via Facebook to check all registration data in the return app. She also asked for the separately registered passengers to be deleted. This provided clarity on the issue, which was discussed at length yesterday. To delete, the name of the person who is concerned should be overwritten with "XXX". Only the name, the other entries can be left unchanged. Sven shared this technological sophistication with his friends, who abstained from comment.

In the morning it was cloudy, but soon the sun came out and brought temperatures above 20 degrees, as every day. After breakfast, they went to the pharmacy and bought six masks for NZ$15. There was a sufficient supply, which was increased daily. From there they went straight on to the supermarket. The queue was very short today, only four or five people stood in front of the entrance. They put on their masks and made a big purchase. Meanwhile, both preferred the regular flight with Qatar Airways, which still seemed reliable. The description about the first and only return flight so far were not very tempting. These considerations played a role in further purchasing planning. More than twice they didn't want to go to the supermarket. The mind told them that the risk of infection was close to zero here, but the virus kept whispering to them that it was nowhere safe. Today the shopping cart was accordingly very full. They paid NZ$110 at the checkout. That should be enough for four days.

Their first booking at the motel has expired today, the second followed seamlessly. They were able to keep the room, only the chip card for the door had to be recoded and they also got some new cards with WI-FI passwords.

In the afternoon, no one was sitting on the porch. Some of the rooms were open, people were lying on the bed inside and looking outside. Inertia had returned, and everyone was helping to reduce the risk of spreading the virus by doing nothing. The television program didn't offer a great variety. Quiz shows, music video clips, talk rounds were not a lucrative offer. Only at the press conferences did they turn it on. Today, 589 people have been reported to have been infected. The number of tests is now about 1,800 per day. The increase remained linear, which was a good sign. The police chief reported the first arrests of people who had repeatedly violated the conditions, but overall, he described the behavior of the population as brilliant.

On the streets around the hotel, a few maniac guys with roaring engines and pounding basses kept passing in their twenty-year-old cars. If the police come to this area, it would be tight for them.

In the late afternoon, Sven spoke to a Scottish pensioner who had been on the road for two months. First in Bali, then Australia and now New Zealand. He would like to stay here if he knew that the isolation would be over in four weeks. He was very concerned about what awaits him in Scotland. Well, he still had time to think, his flight was not booked until April 15.

The message remained invisible today, as did the Facebook group. They waited, but didn't know exactly for what. In the evening, a rumor arose. Tomorrow, March 31 at 9 p.m., an Air New Zealand plane is scheduled to fly via Vancouver to Frankfurt. In fact, the flight with the number NZ6040 was also on the web side of Auckland Airport under the heading "Departures". But it could just as well be a quite normal charter flight to Canada, because the final airport, if it was Frankfurt, was not displayed.

Tuesday, March 31, 2020

Auckland. New Zealand Day 6 Corona Alert Level 4.

Today they had breakfast late and enjoyed the fantastic weather on the veranda. It was already 15 degrees warm in the morning. A beautiful day lay ahead of them.

A phone call of the German Foreign Minister Heiko Maas and his New Zealand counterpart was reported on Facebook. One was looking for a solution, it was read there. It was one of so many insubstantial information. The embassy presented a new article on its website this morning. It said that flights were likely to remain suspended beyond March 31, as no amicable solution had yet been reached with the New Zealand government. In the early afternoon, Prime Minister Ardern said she would comment on the matter at the press conference, as the deadline for presenting the strategy expired today.

Today they took a 2-hour walk through another part of the nature reserve. They walked along a bay where there was no water because of the low tide. You could see a few birds. Now around noon, like every day, there were a few other stranded people on the way who enjoyed the bright sunshine and now 24 degrees. On the way back, they passed a bakery. The scent of fresh bread was still above the property, even though it had been closed for almost a week. A sensory illusion? Bakeries and butchers were not part of essential services, so they were not allowed to open their business.

The press conference began 30 minutes late. That was unusual. Today, there would be 647 infected in New Zealand, still a significant but linear increase. The problem of leaving for Germany as well as other European countries were only briefly touched. Support is given to this project, but the strategy presented is not sufficient. It will take some more time. That was certainly not good news. Later in the parking lot, the anger was expressed more clearly than yesterday. There was no understanding of the delay again.

Stranded person-1: Which game is played with us?

Stranded person-2: Does Mrs. Ardern have a problem with Germany?

Stranded person-3: Are tourists being kept as a stimulus for the hotel industry in the country?

These were the conjectures that have now been debated. It was difficult for foreigners to assess whether the parliament in New Zealand still played a role. It was obvious, however, that the press and other media supported Mrs. Ardern's course in full scale.

The international comparability of the figures was still not available. On the one hand, the criteria were completely different, and on the other hand, they were also not transparent within some countries, including Germany. As a way, it became increasingly difficult to form an opinion on the adequacy of decisions.

Friend-1: This is no different in Europe.

Friend-2: Now is the time for governments. All outperform each other by adopting restrictive measures. If Parliament is still being asked, it is a super-rapid pace. More an alibi engagement than an institution that can thoroughly debate hastily submitted bills.

An hour later, there was suddenly a lot of noise in the motel's yard. Six to eight people walked back and forth loudly palavered. Then two police vehicles came, out of one of them wool blankets and huge plastic bags full of clothes were thrown next to a tree on the ground. The loud shouting people grabbed the things and stormed into Sven and Lings neighboring rooms. Apparently, homeless people had been housed here so that they could also get the chance to self-isolation. A little later, the police had long since left, people, dressed only in a towel, jumped around in the parking lot. They had all enjoyed a refreshing shower, probably the first in a long time.

Sven and Ling left their doors closed in the afternoon and watched the situation through the window, as did the foreigners. The newcomers looked slightly threatening. So, they missed the evening walk.

On Facebook, dubious journalists appeared, allegedly working for renowned newspapers. It was obvious that these were people who weren't working for serious media. Sven urged the group members to be careful, but many posted private sensitivities without hesitation.

On WhatsApp, he discussed issues such as transparency, case numbers, causes of death and the observation that in weeks ago strong democracies had been deprived of essential liberty rights by their governments.

The number of people infected in Germany has been climbing consistently. There were now nearly 71,800, he found no statistics on the number of tests performed, patients in hospital and in the intensive care unit. Sven saw today for the first time that German media reported on the stranded people in New Zealand.

Wednesday, April 1, 2020

Auckland. New Zealand Day 7 Corona Alert Level 4.

The latest news on Facebook came from the embassy this morning. Sven read that many agencies are trying to meet the government's requirements, but it is not yet possible to say when these efforts will be successful. Why were such content-less messages published? They didn't reassure anyone anyway.

The perseverance made sluggish, after a week, there was no news to discover. So, it was hardly surprising that no one could be seen at the door at 10 o'clock. Sleeping two hours longer shortened the waiting time. The cleaning women had adjusted to this.

Sven and Ling took a short walk through a few other streets of the freight forwarding area today and filled up their drinks supplies.

After the noise last night and in the early morning, Sven complained to the motel management about the behavior of the homeless people forcibly housed by the state yesterday. The owners of the motel had no influence on it, they didn't even know the names of their new guests, he learned. Others had already contacted the reception as well. An hour later, a young man came from a health department and explained to the people in very gentle terms what self-isolation and lockdown means. They listened to him in silence, nodding their heads, showing approval. After he was gone, barely a quarter-hour had passed, they continued as before. They were constantly hanging together in a large group, both in the parking lot, in the room or on the veranda. Now there were more than 10 people, because in the evening a few more had been added. They walked around in front of the open doors of the other guests, did not keep a 50-centimeter distance and, moreover, made a noise of hell. Sven did not believe that today's instructions had made a difference. If not, Ling and he agreed, they wanted to change the room or even the hotel the next day.

Mrs. Ardern said in her daily press conference that she would comment on the repatriation program tomorrow. For the statistics, she reported a moderate increase to 708 infected persons and for the first time the number of now recoveries was also reported. It's 90 people. An end to Alert Level 4 is a long way off, she said. No one should hope for short-term easing.

The hours were sticky as porridge. It was hot. Another day less. Not long until April 7. Six days after German, five days after Chinese counting. As expected, there was no new information in the evening. Sven had asked the editorial staff of his hometown newspaper if she was interested in a situation report. The answer arrived tonight. Tomorrow he wanted to get to work and write an article. In the meantime, many other friends and acquaintances in Germany had learned about the return flight program and inquired about the state of affairs here on the ground.

In the evening, the embassy wrote on its website that the registration data should be supplemented again, and fields had been added again. Sven knew this long ago, because the Facebook community had already posted it hours before. The embassy also said it would have to send lists of the data to a New Zealand ministry tomorrow. It seemed anything but digital. One might have been able to call in a professional travel manager, he thought, and other stranded people said the same thing.

Today, all the Americans who had lived here had flown home. The remaining were mostly Germans, along with the Spanish couple, the Scottish pensioner and the Maori group.

Most of the questions in the Facebook groups, by now a second one, were still about the problem of how fellow passengers should be recorded. Many wanted to fly together. Parents with children or older couples were among them. Others would also be happy with separate flights, but it was still not possible to enter what kind of passengers they were. On the website of the embassy, it was again asked to indicate superfluous double registrations by overwriting the name with "XXX". Sven was sure that all the planning was now done with Excel lists.

In Germany, the number of people infected has now been given as 77,900. It would take a while for the measures to take effect. A friend wrote that there is now a detailed discussion about the protective masks in everyday life. Listen, listen, Sven replied, as we know, theses masks were completely unnecessary until recently. Some people see it differently now, was the answer. The mayor of Jena, a German city in Thuringia, yesterday made protective masks compulsory. Long live federalism.

Thursday, April 2, 2020

Auckland. New Zealand Day 8 Corona Alert Level 4.

The people next door behaved a little quieter than on the first night. But already at 7 o'clock in the morning they were again in the 8-pulk together in front of the rooms. They still did not want to understand what self-isolation meant in a "bubble". The morning was sunny and warm, then the first clouds rose. Sven wrote the article for his home newspaper. He then discussed with the reception whether they could move to another apartment in order to keep their distance from these people. But the motel was fully booked. So, they will wait to stay in room 820 until they fly out.

Around noon they set off for another long hike. It led first back to Puketutu Island, but this time on its north side. A few cyclists were there as well, but hardly any pedestrians. It was very monotonous to have to go similar or the same ways, but there were no alternatives. Hundreds of ducks, swans and seagulls roamed the shallow waters of the lagoon. They watched them for a long time.

The number of people infected had risen again somewhat more, to 797, he heard in the afternoon. However, there were now also suspected cases added. These are people with a negative test, but they are classified accordingly due to symptoms and contacts with infected persons. For the first time, the number of cured persons is higher than that of the newly infected. This is also an indicator of the success of the lockdown. The press conference began with these statements. This was followed by the decisive news for foreigners: the government now supports in principle the implementation of return flights. In addition, transfers to the airport are possible by flight, bus or car. The condition for this is that the relevant passengers have a valid ticket with departure within the next twenty-four hours. In addition, Qatar Airways, as the only remaining commercial airline, is allowed to set up a second aircraft to Doha every day. This, too, will provide additional capacity. This was good news for Sven and Ling in that they were now more likely to expect their flight to take place on April 7. After the news became known, countless posts in the Facebook groups followed. Great relief was the basic tenor. Soon after, speculation ensued as to when the flights would start. The first concerned voices could also be heard. They came from the people who were several hundred kilometers from one of the two airports and did not have their own vehicle.

Some local beatniks no longer took the curfew very seriously. As in the last evenings, they roamed the streets at a brisk pace with squeaky tyres and loud music. No one stopped them. That was their way of compensating. At night, their new neighbors were reasonably calm.

On the New Zealand evening, the German morning, WhatsApp messages go back and forth again. That, too, had become a ritual. Sven took up the topic again with the masks. He translated the Chinese version of this dilemma as follows:

"When wearing masks becomes compulsory everywhere, there is no longer any human rights; if no one wears a mask, there are no more people; when everyone wears a mask, there will be no more masks (tomorrow)."

Friend-2 answered spontaneously: I don't have a mask, and there's none to buy. Problem solved! That was the end of the discussion.

Friend-1 took up another point: the German media criticizes the fact that there are still no checks on entry at airports, not even in cases of suspicion. Do we have to understand that?

Sven replied: I think this has been necessary since mid-January. It is irresponsible, a major failure of the German Government and authorities.

They also exchanged views on the number of tests. New Zealand published the exact number daily, in Germany it was obviously rather estimated because there was no central reporting system. However, the tests per million inhabitants appear to be somewhat the same in both countries. Finally, they found that while health and life seemed to be the primary goal of all measures, more and more targets were added, especially economic ones. This made it much more difficult to solve the problem. At the end of the day, Sven read a detailed statement from the New Zealand Tourism Association, which praised Mrs. Ardern for releasing the return flights. After all, it would be fatal if tourists who are now stranded avoided New Zealand in the future. Tourism makes a decisive contribution to prosperity.

Friday, April 3, 2020

Auckland. New Zealand Day 9 Corona Alert Level 4.

In the morning Sven found an e-mail from the newspaper editor. He called his article excellent and would publish it immediately. By now, the embassy had written to all the people who could already fly back today. Air New Zealand flight NZ1960 will depart at 4:30 p.m. and fly via Vancouver to Frankfurt. Only yesterday the act was approved and today they started, which was noticeably fast. On Facebook it was pretty quiet in the morning, as well as in the motel. Of the people stranded here, no one had been selected for the first flight.

Sven and Ling went to the pharmacy again and bought another ten masks. The price was unchanged at NZ$2.50 per unit. They put on one when they arrived at the supermarket. The queue was extremely long today, stretching over three streets, but the wait lasted no longer than twenty-five minutes. People were more likely to stay four meters apart than two meters apart. They bought everything they needed for the remaining four days and evenings, and once again they did not want to run here.

They missed the daily 1 p.m. press conference of the Director of the National Institute of Health, but it was available on the Internet at any time. 868 people are now infected, more than 100 of them already cured, he said. For the 3 p.m. press conference there would be a concrete division of labor from now on, it was announced. From Mondays to Thursdays, it will be held by the Prime Minister, and Friday and Sunday will be taken over by the Finance Minister. There was no one on Saturday. As expected, today was about economic and fiscal aspects of the pandemic. The return flight program was not the subject of any observations or questions raised by the journalists. The decision had been taken, now it was a matter of the implementation and that was the responsibility of the embassy and the airlines. On the part of the embassy there were no new information, also in the Facebook groups there was not a single new post. There was no information on the flights on Air New Zealand's website. New Zealand was still missing on the Lufthansa side, where all the flights of the global return program were listed.

Their housemates from New Zealand behaved now at times ghostly quiet and stayed in their rooms, only to suddenly let off steam again in large groups of eight to twelve people together. They also got frequent visits and continued to care a dirt around level 4. Sven searched the website of the police, where citizens should report violations of the orders. He described the situation in factual terms and asked for these people to be re-instructed.

Tonight, they were cooking delicious-tasting lamb, the first time during their lockdown. Suddenly, dynamic joined the two Facebook groups. It was reported that Lufthansa aircrafts were to depart daily from Christchurch from April 6 and from Auckland from April 7, initially until April 10 inclusive. Now people who had already got a seat for tomorrow's flight with Air New Zealand came forward, even though it could not be found on the usual flight portals. Also, for the 5th of April, emails have already arrived. It was not yet clear which criteria were used to determine the criteria. The emails with the flight tickets now came directly from the airline. On the part of the embassy there were no new statements at all today, also their homepage remained unchanged. A few days ago, Sven and Ling would have loved to get on one of the first best return planes, now they hoped they would not be considered before April 7. Those who did not take up their seat had forfeited their chance, which was communicated as a rule. The status on Qatar still said that their flight will be operated on April 7. Weighing the alternatives became a balancing act, with a return flight becoming more and more a theoretical alternative.

The first return flight with Air New Zealand took-off as planned in the late afternoon. So, the action started. 350 of the more than 10,000 stranded were in the air.

In the evening, Sven learned that his article had been published today. Then he read that Germany had overtaken China with 91,200 infected people, and that Spain was on the verge of surpassing Italy. Even at home, it was known that the flights had begun.

Friend-1: When will you be able to fly?

Sven: We haven't got any tickets yet. It is decided at short notice from flight to flight who is allowed to fly with the next plane.

Friend-2: Our Minister of the Interior apparently plans to quarantine all travelers arriving in Germany for a fortnight.

Sven: Please just don't. I trust that the thorough preparation for this will take longer and that this measure has not yet been implemented on the day of our arrival.

At night, heavy marijuana smells penetrated through the window.

Ling: Amsterdam!

Sven: What do you mean?

Ling: Well, Amsterdam smells like that. But this here is a poor quality.

Saturday, April 4, 2020

Auckland. New Zealand Day 10 Corona Alert Level 4.

Last night's marijuana use had its effect. Only after 10 o'clock did the Maoris wake up and sneak over the yard almost silently, but this changed drastically again in the afternoon. The lady from northern Germany had been given a place on the reserve list for today's flight. In a wise foreboding, she had already returned her car yesterday. Her mood was neutral, although she could be optimistic, because on yesterday's flight apparently 50 people were taken from the reserve list. There were probably a lot of people booked on the flight who were not in Auckland and therefore had not managed to arrive at the airport in time.

Sven: In addition to cases of hardship, why aren't those who are already at the airport flown out first? Logistically, this would be the simplest option, especially since hotel accommodations would then be freed up, which could be used by those who are even further away.

Other stranded people: Consent!

Sven and Ling took another walk, finding another way to go around the Mangere Lagoon. Again, they met a few cyclists, but encounters with walkers were even rarer than on the previous days. The daily routines were always according to the same ritual, only the duration of the walks varied a little. On the street it was also very empty, which was probably because today was Saturday. Sven has been observing for some time that Saturday was the quietest day of the week. Even in the small grocery store, where they filled up the water supplies again, hardly anyone could be seen.

The Air New Zealand plane had departed at 4 p.m. today. Again, apparently all the people who were on the reserve list were brought along, there were even seats left, it was later read on Facebook. In the afternoon, half of the Germans present gathered for a chat. They talked about everything that there was nothing more to say about. Conversation content repeated. Around 5 p.m., a number of Facebook messages were sent concerning the Air New Zealand flight NZ1960 tomorrow, Sunday. So, another plane would fly to Frankfurt tomorrow via Vancouver. Everything indicated that it would now go on strike and soon everyone would have a seat. Initial comments were read in which people told that they had both a confirmed Qatar Airways flight and had received a ticket for a return flight for the same day. They are looking for advice on which plane they should take. The answers were clear:

Take the Qatar machine!

Sven added: The risk of cancellation is now extremely low, and there is no refund of the ticket for short-term cancellations.

Virus: Are you sure that your wife's entry will really work?

He hadn't dealt with it for several days, but now that the return flight was getting closer and closer, the worry was back.

Sven: There is no realistic reason for rejection at the border.

Virus: You know for yourself that you still have doubts.

Tonight, they ate two large rump steaks, the last potatoes they still had were fried.

In the evening, the embassy published a long letter to the "Dear Compatriots". It described the activities of the last few days. This was followed by an apology for the confusion in the allocation of tickets for the first flights. Then there was an invitation to put a check mark on "need-no-return flight" in the return app after arriving at home. This was obviously the only information the organizers could find out about who was already at home. At the end of the letter there was a promise that the procedure had now equipoised and that everything would be much more relaxed and transparent for the days to come. We will see, Sven thought, and turned to other information. Surprisingly, a Condor B767 appeared as one of the return planes. It was supposed to fly people from Auckland to Frankfurt in a few days. Well, that's going to be fun to be squeezed twenty-four hours in the super-tight Condor seats. Sven desperately hoped that this cup would pass them by.

During the night, time was also changed in New Zealand, but in contrary to Germany. Here was winter time, so the clock was turned back an hour. They had once again come an hour closer to home, the time difference was only ten hours.

In addition to studying the figures for those infected, today there were 950 in New Zealand and 96,000 in Germany, further statistics could now be analyzed. A hard-working Facebook user had collected and posted data about the return flights. These included date, airline, departure time, aircraft type and seat capacity. As a total, he already reported 1,060 passengers who were back home today. A good service, praised Sven.

One hour of the evening belonged again to the WhatsApp message exchange.

Friend-1: From the day after tomorrow, the wearing of masks while shopping and on public transport becomes mandatory in Jena, the first municipality in Germany.

Friend-3: Donald Trump also shows first sympathies for the masks. The RKI is now indifferent, at least no longer strictly negative as it has been in the past. It wouldn't hurt in doubt, maybe.

Sven: I read that the masks are now often called mouth-nose protection.

Friend-2: There it is again, the German preference for exact terms.

Sunday, April 5, 2020

Auckland. New Zealand Day 11 Corona Alert Level 4.

They didn't have the opportunity to sleep a little longer because of the time change, their neighbors took care of it. They had probably given up their marijuana last night and were all the more vocal about the new day. All the people here were greeted by a blue sky, garnished with a few white clouds, as if they had just been taken from the washing machine. Even the weather brought no change in the monotony of perseverance. Anyway, the sky turned blue and it was warm, the hours of waiting were rather grey. Their immediate neighbors, a young couple from Xanten on the Lower Rhine, moved back today to the neighboring hotel where they had been a few days ago. Because of the better Wi-Fi, they said. The Spanish couple's room was empty, they were probably heading for Europe with Qatar Airways yesterday. Apart from the Germans, the only other foreigner was the Scottish pensioner. He retreated, changing only a few words with the others. He never seemed tense, he seemed to be one of the people who simply waited, because he had no influence on his current fate anyway.

Throughout the morning, the unbearable noise of the Maori continued. Sven learned from the management of the motel that one of them had been taken away by the police this morning towards the detention. Security people had been on the premises for three nights from 10 p.m. to 6 a.m. But on the day the party went on. For these people, Corona and lockdown was probably the best they had experienced in a long time.

The key messages in today's press conference were:

We have linear growth, although there are now significantly more than 3,000 tests carried out daily.

We have acted significantly earlier than others, especially Europe and the United States. This did not sound without pride.

The vast majority of the population behaved in an exemplary manner.

However, Mrs. Ardern made it clear, using a few examples, that infringements would result in a court ruling within four hours. In addition, risk sports have been removed from the list of fitness activities still allowed. This included canoeing and swimming in the sea.

The day dragged on tenaciously from hour to hour. Sven and Ling went over to count hours instead of days. On Facebook, the same questions kept coming up. Who had received an email for the flight tomorrow, the day after tomorrow, on Wednesday? Maybe I'm not on the list? Did I do anything wrong when registering? Why were people with good health, no young children and no financial constraints allowed to fly and we, the family with 2 young children, the au pair girls without money, the pensioners with urgent need for medical treatment still do not? This were real concerns, and the message that everyone was going to get there didn't help. Everyone has been here for too long, partly because of the government's late turnaround.

Tonight, the two Facebook groups posted new messages from relieved people who had received tickets for Wednesday's flights. Sven had been a little more intensive with Germany for a long time, asked practical questions, wanted to know what was allowed, tolerated and was definitely forbidden. He learned that Deutsche Bahn was apparently still running, but that purely private car journeys outside the residential environment were no longer permitted.

An Air Zealand flight took off from Auckland today. The B777 transported 350 more people to Germany, a country where the number of people infected had exceeded the 100,000 mark. In New Zealand, the number of daily new infections had decreased significantly. The official total was 1,039. It became increasingly apparent that the right measures had been taken. The friends at home reported that there was no agreement within Germany on the criteria for the number of Corona deaths to be collected. Across countries, there would not even be a minimum level of statistical comparability within the EU. Who was surprised?

Monday, April 6, 2020

Auckland. New Zealand Day 12 Corona Alert Level 4.

Around 3 a.m., numerous emails arrived again, as Sven was able to read on Facebook. On the part of the embassy, some people were asked to confirm their registration data. Others were urged not to do so because their data had already been passed on to one of the two airlines. Of course, this caused new uncertainty, even fear among those who, like Sven and Ling, still had not heard anything, neither from the embassy nor from either of the two air lines. Could you really be sure of being on the list? What was the purpose of this action? Confirm without changing content? Should there possibly dragged lists that were sorted over the date of the last change to filter the still large number of people waiting?

Today there was no flight from Auckland to Frankfurt, but tomorrow the first Lufthansa plane was to go out. It would soon arrive in Auckland. Instead, a plane took off from Christchurch, the airport for the stranded on the South Island.

Another waiting couple at their motel had been getting tickets for Wednesday. A young woman from Ulm flew with Qatar Airways today. Sven and Ling's flight was already ready for online check-in, which also worked smoothly. Sven had the check-in confirmations printed at the reception. However, the boarding passes could not yet be issued, which was not surprising, as Ling's documents, residence permit and residence certificate had to be checked at the check-in counter at the airport.

Sven: Keep your fingers crossed that we will skip this last little hurdle.

Ling: Why do you keep having so many concerns? Of course, all will go well.

The two took one last walk in the enclosure. It led long-known paths. Suddenly they discovered a 500-metre-long path that did not know. They, of course, incorporated it into their walk. Thus, the road network here was really completely provided with their footprints. Eventually, they bought another 10 masks. The price was unchanged at NZ$2.50 per unit. The afternoon dragged on. Although it was now only a few hours, it was precisely this waiting period that became a felt eternity.

Most of their Maori neighbors had to leave the motel this morning. With full bags they moved to somewhere else. Only three who had behaved properly all the time were allowed to stay, says the manager of the motel. He did not know where the others were taken by the police.

The butcher from Flensburg, who also lived on their floor with his wife, was no longer there, although no flight departed today. No one knew where they had gone, probably going to another hotel, Sven suspected. Their former neighbors from the Lower Rhine came for a visit in the afternoon. They received the news today that they should no longer update their registration data. That meant they could expect a ticket in the next two or three days. No further news arrived today. Sven suspected that all flights had now been allocated until April 9 and that they wanted to wait until the remaining data was updated. They packed up a few things, grabbed two steaks and, after four days, finally sat on the porch with a glass of wine.

Today's press conference was not of great importance to Sven. There are now 1,106 infected people in New Zealand. It is always better to understand and follow up the individual cases exactly, so one is cautiously optimistic. But the road is still long and it should not even be thought of leaving it even a meter away. These were Mrs. Ardern's messages. There were now 103,400 cases in Germany. Although this was significantly less than in Italy or Spain, these figures now moved to a range where 500 more or less were not taken into account. The differences in the figures reported by JHU and the RKI were no longer relevant.

Tuesday, April 7, 2020

Auckland. New Zealand Day 13 Corona Alert Level 4.

During the night, the news remained calm. In the early morning, some people reported their check-in on the Lufthansa flights. A Boeing 747 took off from Christchurch today and an Airbus 380 took off from Auckland. In addition, there was an Air New Zealand aircraft from both locations. Many had already arrived at home. They wrote about the allocation of seats, especially who was allowed to sit in business class. It was not always the ones who deserved it because of their state of health. There had been no scramble at check-in, because with the allocation of the tickets the seats had already been allocated as well. There were also reports of the meagre service on board, but no one wanted to see this as a criticism. Everyone was just happy to be at home. The scenes in the arrivals area of Frankfurt Airport were described with horror by many. First of all, there were no health checks, no temperature measurement, not even with an infrared camera. After the baggage was handed out, 350 people stood outside and waited for 350 arrivals. It was hugged, kissed, all the rules of distance were forgotten. In New Zealand, no one was really exposed to the risk of infection, but arrived here on German the risk was not low. This was in the right way with the decision of the Federal Cabinet, according to which from April 10 all arriving passengers had to go into domestic quarantine. Apart from the fact that this was ordered far too late, since 180,000 people were already back, the reason could only be that one was really in danger of getting infected on arrival. Sven did not read this news any further. Tomorrow they would experience by themselves what is going on in Frankfurt.

In the early morning, after restless sleep, he read the entry rules for Germany once more and took screenshots of it in case there was a discussion with the police. Everything looked like a trouble-free process. There were still many familiar faces in the motel when they boarded the shuttle bus to the airport at 11 a.m. They were farewelled with "Please come back under better circumstances", after 13 days. A truly long stay in an airport motel. In front of the International Terminal it was empty, no further flights were running throughout the afternoon and the Lufthansa plane had already departed, albeit 90 minutes late. The check-in area was intended exclusively for Qatar Airways flight QR921. At the entrance to the terminal, the passports and tickets were checked, and inside only one in two counters were opened in order to be able to keep the 2-meters distance during the procedure. Already three hours before departure, a long queue had formed, but without any hustle and bustle it was handled in a friendly and thorough manner. More than 70% were young people under 30. Some with surfboard, wakeboard, guitars and large backpacks. They were people who had not only been in New Zealand for three weeks. The copy of Ling's residence permit was the key to her departure. Without this document, Germany would not have allowed entry, and the airlines knew that. A Qatar Airways employee took a photo of the document for their own papers. Then they had the boarding passes in their hands. Infinite relief.

Sven (on the virus): That's it for you. Stay here, your days to unsettle us are over. I'll watch from home how they're going to wipe you out here.

Virus: I have brothers and sisters in Germany. You won't escape us that quickly.

Sven didn't notice. The ease was back. Passport control and security check were done at lightning speed, there were no passengers on other flights. All shops and lounges were closed. High white barriers had been erected to conceal the shop windows. A ghostly atmosphere accompanied each of their steps. At 12 o'clock opened a small kiosk selling non-alcoholic drinks, sandwiches, nuts and fruit. On the way to the departure gate, they saw a SWISS plane and the Lufthansa

A380. They were parked on the apron, waiting for the flights tomorrow morning. Their B777 was at gate 6, all the other gates were empty. The machine was occupied to the last seat. On time, they took off for a flight that would take 17 1/2 hours. When the plane left New Zealand and headed for the Tasman Sea soon after, wistfulness arose. What had happened in the last few weeks? Were there really only 5 weeks? A huge change in everyday life, in a sense from one hour to the next. And in Germany, everyday life would no longer be as they knew it before they left.

They flew over Australia far to the south. There were initially some turbulences but it was not an unpleasant flight. The service on board was excellent, the seats comfortable and the staff extremely friendly. They thought for a moment about the flight conditions in the repatriation planes and were thankful that Qatar Airways had not stopped operating like all other airlines. They landed in Doha at 11:15 p.m. local time. Here, too, many shops were closed, but a number of flights from Australia and Asian countries arrived at night, and a few hours later there were numerous connections to European cities.

Relaxed, they waited for their onward flight to Frankfurt. The view of WhatsApp and the internet messages shortened the time. New Zealand were still on the winning track, 1160 infected cases, an increase of 54 on the day they left. Germany reports 107,700. It was also interesting to read that the New Zealand Health Minister had violated the "Stay Home" demand. He had chauffeured his children to a beach 20 kilometers from his house and had been caught doing so. The police reported the violation properly. Mrs. Ardern said that in normal times she had fired him immediately, but now he had to do his job. The situation is too serious to waste even one day of personnel debates.

In Germany, an FDP politician had boasted in the press that he had intervened directly at the embassy in Wellington because of his good relations with the Foreign Office, and the next day four people from his constituency were already sitting in a repatriation plane. Even in this way, priorities could be controlled, Sven thought, remained relaxed and made himself comfortable in an armchair.

Wednesday, April 8, 2020

Traveling. New Zealand Day 14 Corona Alert Level 4.

During the four-hour wait at Doha Airport, Sven read the latest posts in the Facebook groups. The focus gradually shifted to the reports of happy home arrivals. They always told about the flights, the special type of service, about the crowds on arrival, about the happiness, despite all the inadequacies, to be in Germany. Some began to ask what the return flight would actually cost. This was not known before departure. However, each passenger had to make a statement pledging to pay the amount set at a later time. Of those still stranded, he read an ever-increasing concern to be forgotten. They were all eagerly waiting for the redemptive message. The third group were those who had received a ticket and whose departure was imminent. Some of them had even been given seats for both flights for the same day, some had tickets issued in a different name, others wanted to know how to get to the airport from their remote accommodation. Yesterday, April 7, four aircrafts had finally departed towards Frankfurt and numerous people on the reserve list were taken with them. There were also a few who were only called an hour before departure because they were registered on a third list which had been set up for those who could be at the airport within 15 minutes after a call. The number of people waiting had thus shrunk by 1,500.

The embassy also appeared again on Facebook and urged anyone who had not heard anything to confirm their data once again. That was already the third or fourth call. It has also been made clear that under no circumstances can everyone be at home at Easter. Sven was curious if he would receive an email.

The Qatar Airways plane from Doha to Frankfurt was also almost fully booked. The flight lasted only a short 5 1/2 hours, then they landed at the Rhein-Main-Airport in Frankfurt. Everywhere parked Lufthansa planes were on the ground, and air traffic had almost come to a standstill. The border policeman thoroughly checked Ling's documents, in particular the copy of the residence permit, and then allowed her to enter. He also provided her with a fact sheet on the virus, informing her of distance rules and hand washing. That was all. They did not hear his voice, he remained mute. German travelers who could use the machine passport control did not even receive this sheet. Why hasn't a temperature been measured here? Why wasn't at least one health questionnaire handed out? Since Terminal 2 was now closed, the aircraft was parked in area B of Terminal 1. Only one more flight, from Helsinki, was delivered to the baggage claim carousels. A lot of people were waiting for their loved ones outside, but there was not the crowd that was reported by the people from the repatriation flights.

They took the train home. The trains were yawning empty, you didn't have to worry about keeping the desired distance. They first made a big purchase so as not to get into a shopping hustle and bustle before Easter. It was also very quiet there. From the 2-meters, which were the measure of the minimum distance in New Zealand, in Germany 1.5-meter became the rule. Can't the viruses fly as far here as they do in the clear air at the other end of the world? In the supermarket, they saw virtually no people wearing a mask. There were also no security personnel to regulate the entrance. Handles of the shopping carts and keyboards for PIN entry were also not cleaned. However, plexiglass windows had been installed at the cash registers to protect the sales staff.

On the first day at home, New Zealand reported 1,210 people infected, 50 more than the previous day. In Germany, there were now 113,300, well over 5,000 new infections in one day. In both countries, about half of the lockdown time was over. In New Zealand, it was already clear how the success came about. In Germany, this was not yet recognizable.

Then they had to recover from the long journey. Over the next few days, they had plenty of time to acclimatize at home and find out how life at home had changed compared to the beginning of March.

Today, China began cautiously to bring Wuhan, the epicenter of the pandemic, back to normal. The lockdown had lasted 76 long days there. Ling was proud of the success of the fight against Corona in her home country.

Lockdown – In Germany

Thursday, April 9, 2020

At home. New Zealand Day 15 Corona Alert Level 4.

Sven continued to listen with interest to the press conferences in New Zealand. Today, everything sounded very confident, although new quarantine measures were to come into force from April 10. All New Zealanders, it was said, who return home, must be in forced quarantine for two weeks. This replaces the current order for self-isolation at home. This quarantine will not take place at home, but in hotels rented by the government. All costs for accommodation and food as well as for necessary medical measures will be borne by the state. Until now, such a strict rule could not have been applied, because the number of people who had returned with 40,000 people had exceeded the capacity of the hotel beds in the country.

The organization of the return flights was fundamentally changed overnight. The embassy urged anyone who had not yet received a return flight ticket to contact the embassy by email. The data in the return app obviously didn't matter anymore. Soon after, there was a supplementary request that anyone who could be at the airport in a few hours should immediately contact the embassy by e-mail. For this purpose, a specific e-mail address had been set up.

Sven and Ling first went to the Civic Office to pick up the eAT card. The only front office employee opened a window to the street through which she handed over the document. It was forbidden to enter the room. Then they went to the bakery and to a fruit farm. Both were open to their astonishment. Already on this first day it was clear that the term lockdown allowed more activities in Germany than in New Zealand. There were a lot more people on the roads and the car traffic was much denser. But direct social contacts with people of other households were forbidden. With the exception of the family members, one could only meet with a maximum of one additional person, with the minimum distance to be respected. So, this was the German version of the New Zealand "bubble".

After many weeks of communication via WhatsApp, they now used the phone much more frequently as a means of exchanging information. After all questions about personal well-being were answered quickly – all of them were, thank God, healthy – a substantive discussion about life with the virus began as expected.

Sven: Let's take a look at a few facts. With the lockdown now in force for two weeks, well below 50 new infections are reported in New Zealand, today there are only 29 new cases, a total of 1,239. The number of tests is already over 51,000, i.e. 2.5% of which are positive. The target of 70% contamination has never been issued in New Zealand. The government is aiming to eliminate the virus, zero new infections at the end of the measures over a longer period of time.

Friend-1: The task of fighting the virus in New Zealand is under-complex.

Sven: Well, the Kiwis have only 1/16 of our population, but also only 1/16 of the resources. The relative amount of work is also a challenge for New Zealand. Crucially, however, the Kiwis acted very quickly, while Germany had been watching and waiting for too long. This has nothing to do with sub-complexity. It will definitely take a few more days to see how successful the measures will be. In any case, they closed the shop three or four weeks earlier than the countries in Europe.

Friend-1: No matter, New Zealand has no land borders, only a minimum of economic interaction, lower population density. Making a connection with Europe is like comparing apples to pears.

Sven: Partly true, but it's not everything. Rugby games have tens of thousands of followers and spectators. They were cancelled much earlier in New Zealand, although that hit the hearts of hundreds of thousands of fans. In Europe, on the other hand, with many more cases, the Champions League and Bundesliga matches with 50,000 spectators continued to take place in the stadium. In New Zealand there are big festivals, all of which have long since been cancelled, but in Germany carnival was celebrated cheerfully and thoughtlessly. Crucially, however, I believe that they have a very large data base due to the considerable number of tests and that the dark figures are already significantly lower than here. In two to three weeks, we will see whether early action is an advantage or ultimately not relevant.

There were also four return flights today. So, the action went very well. The number of people infected continued to rise sharply, relatively speaking, absolutely anyway. In New Zealand on 1,239, in Germany on 118,200.

Friday, April 10, 2020

At home. New Zealand Day 16 Corona Alert Level 4.

Sven's head was much freer than at the time of the lockdown in New Zealand. It wasn't the fear of the virus. He never had this, and even here in Germany it had not come up. In New Zealand, it was simply the concern that, in an extreme situation, there was no room for independent action. Here in the familiar environment, it was much easier to make the decisions he thought were appropriate if necessary. The virus no longer spoke to him. Its German brothers and sisters, with whom it had said goodbye on the day of departure in Auckland, were not present. Equally, Corona continued to determinate almost the whole life. But the lockdown in New Zealand was so formative for him that he didn't miss a day to deal with the development there.

The number of people infected in New Zealand had risen again somewhat more. Confirmed and probable cases increased by 44 to 1,283 at the other end of the world. Today there was no press conference, the Good Friday was a very important holiday in New Zealand. On this day, unlike Easter Sunday and Easter Monday, the shops remained closed and political life, if that was possible now at all, disappeared from view for a day. Divine services did not take place, because churches were closed in Alert Level 4. The second death was reported. A woman over 90 with a slew of age-related illnesses died two days after a positive test. Also, in New Zealand no distinction was made between died "of" and died "with" Corona. It was absurd how the Corona deaths were counted.

In Germany, the quarantine obligation came into force today for all those who entered by land, water or air. At the airport, the returnees were given a note on which they could read that they had to report to their local health department. There they would learn how the quarantine would actually take place. It was to be assumed that there was no uniform regulation.

While walking, Sven and Ling noticed that the Germans behaved in the same way as the New Zealanders. They kept their distance from each other when they passed others. Their first experiences with cyclists, on the other hand, were quite opposite. They were much more numerous than in New Zealand, remained stubbornly on their trail and drove past oncoming pedestrians even at a distance of only 50 centimeters.

The lockdown in Germany still did not seem to have had great success. Among those tested, there were again 4,000 newly infected.

The embassy announced that the last return plane would take off on April 14. Sven was very curious to see if he would ever receive personal information. The return campaign, however, continued in the usual density.

Saturday, April 11, 2020

At home. New Zealand Day 17 Corona Alert Level 4.

The countdown of the return flights had begun. Flights from Christchurch were scheduled for two more days. The flight from Auckland was to be flown on three more days, then the action would be completed. Seats have now been allocated without exception to those who contacted the embassy directly by e-mail. On the last flights there had been a very large number of no-shows, so that some seats remained vacant, despite the reserve list.

The embassy informed that one should now come to the airport without a formally issued ticket. If the police check, it is sufficient to provide the e-mail communication with the diplomatic mission abroad, because it is sufficiently documented that one is registered for the return action.

Sven and Ling got on their bikes for a tour of the vicinity. Finally, a change to the daily walks. A lot of people were on the road today in glorious early summer weather. On the narrow bike paths there was hardly any opportunity to keep to the required 1.5-meter distance. In the next few days, they would therefore give up cycling. It was still unclear to what extent the car was allowed to be used. However, it seemed to be unproblematic to go to places that were further away from the place of residence, for example, to hike there. Nowhere was this formulated as precisely as in New Zealand.

Today, both countries reported figures indicating the success of the strict measures. Twenty-nine cases were added in

New Zealand, bringing the total to 1,312. The number of people reported as having recovered from COVID-19 had now significantly exceeded that of those who were actively infected. A decrease in new infections has also been recorded in Germany. With 2,700 new cases, the total number was now 124,900.

Sunday, April 12, 2020

At home. New Zealand Day 18 Corona Alert Level 4.

Easter Sunday. In Germany there was a lot going on in the wonderful weather. Cars, motorcycles, walkers, cyclists. Wherever you looked, people were on the streets. Sven guessed how quiet it was on these holidays in New Zealand. Even if you wanted to, in many cases it was not possible to keep to the 1.5-meter distance. Cyclists in particular were quite unconcerned, as they saw yesterday. Sven was sure that the requirement to keep distance made only a limited sense if one allowed almost unlimited leisure activities at the same time.

The embassy said that due to a lack of demand, the last return planes would go out on April 13. No more tickets were issued, no more e-mails were sent. If you wanted to fly, you should come to the airport. The ticket was guaranteed. Pragmatism had prevailed.

New Zealand reported the lowest number of new infections since the lockdown began. Only 18 had joined, bringing the total to 1,330. However, this very positive news was put into perspective by the fact that there was significantly less testing over the Easter weekend days.

China, the country where the virus first appeared in huge degree, communicated its concrete plans to open schools, universities and businesses. Everything will take place between the end of April and mid-May. The school leaving examinations were postponed by four weeks. The educational institutions were closed for a total of three months. How long would it take in Germany? Sven heard a lot of complaints and worries after less than four weeks. There were also new encouraging figures for Germany. 127,000 infected on Easter Sunday, after an increase of 2,100. Everyone knew that the Easter effect, i.e. fewer tests, should not be forgotten. Politicians, on the other hand, use these figures to shower themselves with praise.

Monday, April 13, 2020

At home. New Zealand Day 19 Corona Alert Level 4.

The last return plane had left Auckland tonight. It was an emotional moment, as the pilot was allowed to fly a loop over the city, whose TV tower was specially illuminated in black, red and golden light, Germanys national colors. It was also the moment when the immediate experience of being stranded with Sven and Ling slowly faded. They had become accustomed to the new reality in Germany. And yet not a day went by when Sven did not deal with New Zealand.

The news in the two Facebook groups had dropped sharply. Numerous expressions of thanks to all those who had helped with the return campaign dominated the posts. The quarantine at home, which has been mandatory for returnees since April 10, was discovered as a new topic. There was confusion about their actual process, which, according to initial reports, seemed to be regulated very differently from a regional level. With the quarantine in New Zealand, none of this bore the slightest resemblance. In addition, initial experiences with the lockdown in Germany were compiled. Opinions were clear. In contrast to New Zealand, things were much more casual.

New Zealand today reported 19 new infected people, reaching 1,349 in total, with more than 3,000 added in Germany, resulting in a total of 130,100.

In their private WhatsApp group, they discussed a Heidelberg lawyer today. The Federal Prosecutor's Office investigated her after announcing that she would appeal to the Federal Constitutional Court against the restriction of fundamental rights. One of the friends took the trouble to study all the ordinances that formed the legal basis for the great restrictions. That was a huge number of documents, because each state had its own set of rules. After all, there was a fairly complete compilation of these on Wikipedia. However, Sven just studied a few of them.

Sven: Let's talk about the intentions of the measures. Is it really hard to be found somewhere about what and how the success of all the actions is measured? Are there quantitative or other criteria or objectives to be achieved, or do the government deliberately allow itself to interpret in order to be able to speak more easily of successes?

Friend-2: I think the doubling time of infections is a good benchmark. At the beginning in Germany and many other countries, this was well under ten days. Today it is twenty days with us, which means that with an average illness duration of twenty days, the situation in the clinics remains as it is now. Even longer doubling times would ease the situation, shorter ones would lead to escalation.

Sven: But I can't read or hear anywhere that's still the government's goal. This was the last time presented in the media that way three weeks ago.

None of them had a clear answer to the question.

Sven: Perhaps the press conference announced for tomorrow will shed light on the dark?

Tuesday, April 14, 2020

At home. New Zealand Day 20 Corona Alert Level 4.

Sven and Ling had the next experience in public space when they went to their post office, which still had quite normal opening hours. Since only two customers were allowed to be indoors at the same time, a queue of more than ten people had formed outside, all of which kept a large distance from each other. But only two of them wore a mask. Sven always had a face mask with him and as soon as he came across a conglomerate of several people, he put it on. Ling, the Chinese woman, did the same, of course. "Mask people" in Germany seemed strange.

The RKI spoke at a press conference. It saw a clear trend towards declining case numbers. There has already been a lot of speculation in the media about easing scenarios, with some journalists calling for them. Tomorrow there will be a video conference with the Chancellor and the leaders of all German provinces, in which the time after the lockdown will be discussed and decisions will be made. The transition to Alert Level 3 was also discussed in New Zealand, but Mrs. Ardern dismissed all speculation about it. The decision will be made next Monday and not a moment earlier. One wants to wait for the case numbers of the coming days.

New Zealand's numbers have been as expected by decision-makers. With only 17 new cases, the total number rose to 1,366, in Germany only 1,100 cases were added. Now it was 131,400 in total. New Zealand increased the number of tests significantly. Not only suspected cases or people with symptoms were tested, but also first samples of employees in supermarkets and nursing homes. The vast majority of the tests were negative, the proportion of positively tested in the total number of tests fell to less than 2%, which was a remarkable number.

Wednesday, April 15, 2020

At home. New Zealand Day 21 Corona Alert Level 4.

The lockdown, although the details vary widely, had led to successes in both countries. In New Zealand, due to the clear objective, it was to be confirmed with concrete figures, in Germany a quantitative measurement of success was difficult because there were no corresponding targets. But both the federal government and all the federal states praised themselves for what they had achieved. As an effective means of convincing the population, they used the method of comparison. They chose other countries where the number of people infected and the Corona deaths was significantly higher: France, Italy, Spain and the United Kingdom. Sven also heard that the interim success was described as fragile. In both countries, details of the forthcoming new phase have now been discussed, it was all about easing. In New Zealand, this was based on the long-established Alert Level definitions, which laid down the scope for easing in principle. In Germany, it seemed to be more of a sequence of individual measurements based on no overarching master plan.

Again, the press conferences made all the difference. In New Zealand, Ardern and Bloomfield announced the measures and described the current situation clearly and precisely in 10 minutes. Forty minutes remained for the journalists. At least 40 to 50 questions pattered on the two every day. They answered each one in a concise and precise manner. Not even one remained vague, none of them talked at cross-purposes. In Germany, four people from the government spoke for a very long time and the question time of the journalists was significantly shorter than the total speaking time of the government representatives. More than five questions could hardly be asked, then the time had run out. If the answer did not refer to the specific question, what often had been the case, it was not asked again by the journalists. They just accepted that their questions had not always been answered.

The Federal Government had adopted guidelines that it gave to the Prime Ministers of the provinces. They would decide in the days after that on the concrete design of the measures. The circle of participants could not yet find agreement to a duty to wear masks, but instead the chancellor urged that masks should be worn voluntarily while shopping and in public transport.

The choice of words also showed how difficult it was to deal with the subject. Instead of simply saying masks, everyone knew what it meant, one of the speakers referred to them as mouth-nose protection, another used the term everyday mask, a third said community mask. The chancellor immediately used all the terms and combined them with the word "or" when she made one of her long-winded statements.

It has also been announced that retail stores with a retail area of up to 800 square meters will be allowed to reopen. Scenarios for the slow opening of kindergartens and schools have been discussed, but not yet decided. However, the contact barrier remained unchanged. All easing measures should come into force on Monday April 20.

The embassy in Wellington wrote on its website that the repatriation operation was now officially over. She gave some statistics. 10,000 people were taken home on 26 flights.

In the morning, the small group of Sven's close friends met today for a virtual meeting via video.

Sven: Which source do you use to view the case statistics?

Friend-1: I use worldometers. There are concrete figures on the infected, the dead, the tests and much more. The whole world is covered and the data is constantly updated.

Friend-2 responded: But if you look at the origin of the data, it's wildly messed up. Press articles, news channel and health ministries are used by worldometers, some of the sources are themselves second-guessers.

Sven: You can play around with the numbers really nicely. I just looked at the number of tests. As a result, 8% of all people tested are infected in Germany, and in New Zealand this figure is less than 2%. Obviously, there are other criteria for who is tested.

Friend-1: That's all relative. There is no uniform systematic counting method. But at least you get an idea. The absolute figures should not be looked at so closely.

Sven: Yes, I agree.

The video meeting ended with the question of whether anyone wanted to give a forecast for the date of their next real meeting. No one dared to make a prediction.

From then on, Sven used this source every day. The data of the JHU were very similar, the RKI was always below. In the large number of cases, however, the differences were no longer significant. For New Zealand there were no differing figures anyway, the authorities published their figures absolutely consistent, once a day. Today, New Zealand announced 20 new cases, bringing the total to 1,386. In Germany, there was an increase of 3,400 cases, resulting in a total of 134,800.

Sven had written a second article yesterday, which dealt with the last days of their being stranded in New Zealand until returning to Germany. The editorial staff of the regional newspaper responds immediately with the promise to publish it the next day.

Thursday, April 16, 2020

At home. New Zealand Day 22 Corona Alert Level 4.

In Germany came the great hour of the province's Prime Ministers. What was declared yesterday as a consensual result of the discussion with the Federal Government has already received a specific coloration in some federal states. A first province imposed a mouth-nose protection obligation.

In New Zealand, Prime Minister Ardern once again made it unequivocally clear that the specific rules and the deadline for Alert Level 3 would not be announced until next Monday.

Today Sven received an email from the New Zealand Ministry of Health. He had asked what was meant by "probable cases", because they were also counted among the infected. The answer was precise. The increase in the figures in New Zealand was as calculated in the optimistic projections. There were 15 new cases, the total number now being 1,401. In Germany, the number of new infections increased by similar values as in the previous days. 2,900 new cases brought the total to 137,700.

In the afternoon there was a short exchange via WhatsApp.

Friend-2: I ordered surgical masks at the pharmacy this morning and just picked them up. 36 euros for 20 pieces.

Sven: In mid-January I already bought a stock of 50 pieces for us. The package cost 20€ at the time. The price develops with scarcity.

Then they came back to talk about the goals of the German lockdown.

Sven: The question of the goal does not go out of my mind. Due to the long stay in New Zealand, I only experienced the development in Germany in fragments. At the beginning of the second week of March, a virologist, on whose assessment our government is probably very keen, spoke of the need of the contamination of the population as a meaningful goal. He did not mention a period of time for this. Mrs. Merkel then reproduced this as a political objective of the government. I once calculated quite conservatively: Even with a five-year period and 60% of the population for contamination, that would be 27,000 people infected per day. This is pure insanity. That would result in hundred thousand of fatal casualties. Soon nothing was heard of this project, it seems to have disappeared as a target in the sinking. Then the target was changed, now it was necessary to significantly extend the doubling time. There is no more to read of this either. Yesterday in the press conference there was no mention of the absolute number of people infected or of the deaths, nor even words of sympathy to family members of those who died of Corona. Reducing these figures is probably not a concrete goal as well, if at all an indirect follow-up. Now the goal seems to be that our health system does not collapse. At least that has probably been achieved so far. Is that really the only objective of all these measures?

Friend-1, he changed the subject: Last night on a talk show there were politicians and virologists who were very skeptical about the planned easing. The easing comes too cumulative and far too soon. It must now be a question of bringing the number of reproductions, i.e. the number of people infected on average by a person who is already infected, to a value of well below 1. The chancellor had also mentioned this as an important new goal. By the way, the Chinese started with relief actions when the value was 0.35.

Sven: The RKI said that this value is now between 0.7 and 0.9. Our risk with a second wave is high, it was said nevertheless. We would have no resources; we should not allow ourselves a failed attempt. The return to the current lockdown measures would lead to great unrest among the population if we let slacken the reins too soon.

These were times when decisions could only be made on the basis of assumptions.

Friday, April 17, 2020

At home. New Zealand Day 23 Corona Alert Level 4.

Finally, a day, without intensive involvement with Corona. The brain also had to switch off once. The only news from

New Zealand was that two people in Auckland had sued Jacinda Ardern in the country's Supreme Court for not deeming the lockdown measures to be appropriate. The action had at least been taken.

In Germany, the overbidding competition between the provinces was fully ignited. Only three days left, until the easing. There was an imaginative way to concretize this. Other federal states imposed a mask requirement. Bavaria increased the number of physical social contacts outside the family from zero to one, thus following the rule that was already in force in all other provinces. In addition, it was determined in detail what kind of retail stores were allowed to open. Sven was sure that this would continue throughout the weekend.

Nevertheless, the daily view of the statistics was not lacking. Eight new cases were found in New Zealand, resulting in a total of 1,409. A further 3,500 cases in Germany arose to 141,400.

Saturday, April 18, 2020

At home. New Zealand Day 24 Corona Alert Level 4.

As is so often the case, Sven was the first to listen to the press conference from New Zealand. It was beneficial to first get concrete and consistent figures on developments over the last twenty-four hours, and then to listen to Mrs. Ardern, who justified her decisions with a confidence-creating voice and content, gave background information and continued to respond to the journalists with knowledge and passion.

In Germany, on the other hand, Sven experienced, almost every minute, how reports from the federal states came up, in an unbelievable dynamic about ever new individual measure. Now the mask obligation had already been ordered in five federal states. In the next week, shopping malls were allowed to open again in some of the provinces, under the strictest conditions in terms of distance keeping.

Personally, Sven and Ling had long since arranged themselves with the restrictions of everyday life. Daily long walks were part of it, they only made a big grocery purchase once a week, public transport they did not use. Two or three times a week they ordered food at one of the local restaurants. Most had been open at least a few days a week and offered food and drinks to pick up. This was their contribution to the local gastronomy not to leave them completely without turnover.

Even today Sven took a look at the statistics. 13 new infections in New Zealand, i.e. 1,422 infected in total. Of these, well over 50% have already been judged to be cured by doctors. This value was recorded according to transparent criteria. In Germany it was appreciated. At home, 1,900 people had been found infected today, the total now being 143,300.

Sunday, April 19, 2020

At home. New Zealand Day 25 Corona Alert Level 4.

It was 8 o'clock in the morning. The recording of the press conference was available on the website of the New Zealand Ministry of Health. Jacinda Ardern went into detail about the follow-up of contacts of infected persons. That, she said, is one of the keys to success. At present, 200 employees within the District Health Boards (DHB) are employed full-time. They worked seven days a week, and made 5,000 calls a day. The government's aim is to identify all contacts within 48 hours in 80% of all cases. They named it the "Golden Standard". Activities included mainly phone calls, but also visits. Tools and apps are helpful as support, but nothing more. Further capacity expansion is already underway. For Sven, this enormous action seemed somewhat oversized, given that it was compared to the few current cases. Ardern also said that so far 1,600 people who have entered from abroad are in the state-managed quarantine. Now, more than a thousand tests are carried out every day in institutions where the workers have intensive contact with people. These included supermarkets, nursing homes and private and state-owned rest homes.

In Germany, there were apparently no statistics on the quarantine required for entry from abroad, which has been in force since April 10. In the German media, the daily case numbers were no longer reported in the first place, they had probably become the norm, had no more spectacular fluctuations. Instead, they found again accusatory articles towards the Middle Kingdom. China was accused of informing the world too late and not comprehensively enough about Corona. The usual reflex to distract from his own failures, Sven thought. As usual, the United States were in the driver's seat for the accusation, as usual, Germany adhered few days later but not as loud as the US.

He noticed again and again that the government, especially the Chancellor, had no regrets about the high death toll and no condoling words from those who remained. The number of deaths and infections, on the other hand, was often used to compare them with other countries such as Italy, France, Belgium and the United Kingdom. From this it was easy to deduce the success of the measures imposed in Germany.

At the end of the day, the figures remained true to the trend. In New Zealand, only nine cases were added. These resulted in a total of 1,431 infected persons. Germany came through the increase from 1,900 cases to 145,200 infected.

Monday, April 20, 2020

At home. New Zealand Day 26 Corona Alert Level 4.

Today, New Zealand announced the key decisions for the next phase. One will move to Alert Level 3, but five days later than initially planned, i.e. on April 28. The reliefs did not go as far as in Germany. Social contacts can be maintained at a minimum, but the principle of the "bubble" would remain in force. Manufacturing, Construction and Forestry are expected to resume operations if safety measures are guaranteed. Schools and kindergartens would be gradually opened, but initially only for children under the age of 10, in order to give their parents more freedom to work. Retailers would be allowed to resume operations, but it would not be allowed to serve customers in the store. Orders would have to be placed online, as would payment. Goods could then be picked up at the store where certain areas would have to be made available. Deliveries were permitted, but they had to be made contactless. According to Ardern, the companies now have one week to prepare their processes and premises in accordance with these rules. Further details would be communicated later in the week. Today, Sven also learned that Mrs. Ardern personally provided the bereaved of the Corona dead her expression of condolences.

Sven and Ling drove to the shopping center near their home. It was, to some extent, an inspection tour to see with their own eyes how the reopening of the shops was shaping up. About half of the shops were open in the afternoon, the number of customers remained small, the 1.5-meter distance was observed, security and control personnel could not be seen. No one wore a mask, not even the sales staff. In the evening, television showed footage from large cities where crowds could be seen on the streets. Who knows if these pictures were real?

Also, today, a number of federal states in Germany were added, which from next week made masks mandatory. However, it is sufficient to tie an ordinary fabric or scarf around. Even simple surgical masks were still not available in sufficient quantities for the population. Similar experiences were also shared by friends from their places: most of the shops were open, even the large ones, as they had divided their sales area in such a way that they did not exceed the permitted area of 800 square meters. There is not much going on, but there is still a jam in front of the ice cream parlors. Masks were not seen at all.

The new case numbers showed the expected values. Again 9 new cases in New Zealand, i.e. 1,440 in total. There were 1,800 new cases in Germany, 147,000 in total.

Tuesday, April 21, 2020

At home. New Zealand Day 27 Corona Alert Level 4.

In New Zealand, the tests have been extended. Samples in schools and remote communities were added. There were only two cases where the origin of the infection could not yet be determined. Contact tracing turned out to be a strength.

In Germany, the countries that had fluctuated until the very end had also brought themselves to force to wear masks, with a slightly different start date. The obligation related to shopping and public transport, only Berlin allowed purchases to continue without a mask. To the chagrin of an entire cult community, the Oktoberfest in Munich was cancelled today. Some courts had allowed smaller demonstrations with up to 50 people. The demonstrators must observe a distance of 1.5-meter among each other and 2-meters from non-participants. Congratulations to the police who should monitor this.

Drones, Sven thought, would be a suitable instrument here. But that was just his personal view of things.

The number of tests carried out, Sven found, was transmitted to the RKI only once a week from the laboratories. In the magazine DIE ZEIT, there was an article about New Zealand's anti-corona measures today. Very matter-of-fact and quite worth reading. On other occasions it was very rare to read about New Zealand, now European media occasionally looked at what the Kiwis are doing to fight the virus.

Sven and Ling wanted to go for a walk in the city park, but it was still closed due to Corona. So, they chose the forest for a hike once more. They then went to two pharmacies, but there were no surgical masks on stock and orders were not possible. The staff did not do more. Sven labeled the possibility of wearing simple fabric masks, scarves or neck scarves as a protection a pure nonsense. Either proper masks or none.

Today, the smallest increases in a long time have been reported. The tests in New Zealand revealed five new cases of infection, i.e. 1,445 in total. Only 1,400 new cases were reported in Germany, the smallest increase in many days, i.e. 148,400 in total. Of course, this relatively low value served as a welcome argument for advocates of further easing.

Wednesday, April 22, 2020

At home. New Zealand Day 28 Corona Alert Level 4.

In New Zealand, businessmen and private individuals learned more details about Alert Level 3, including about travel guidelines and leisure activities. In summary, it could be said that shorter journeys by car would be possible within the region. You could swim, surf, go fishing and a lot more, but there was a requirement to practice only the sports you master already. It is not the time to learn something new now.

It was Wednesday, time for Sven's virtual meeting with his friends. For two hours, they debated the medical, economic and social aspects of COVID-19, as well as the deprivation of freedoms, fundamental rights and federal competences. They were also unsure when they could meet legally in person again. In any case, it was still not allowed under the current contact rules. Issues that had nothing to do with Corona were not the subject of their debate.

The Administrative Court in Hamburg had declared the 800 square meters rule inadmissible for retail. Large furniture stores and electronics stores reopened because they found a creative solution for space limitation. In the talk shows, people met who judged the opening measures as going too far and those who wanted to open much more. The talk show guests sat with a great distance to each other, some were connected by video, there were no audiences in the studio. No one wore masks, but when the question came, one was quickly conjured out of the jacket pocket. Rarely a surgical mask, often one tailored by the dear relatives, one even in Bavarian white-blue.

In New Zealand, the number of new infections remained constant below 10. The total number increased to 1,451 by 6 new cases, and more than 5,000 tests were carried out today. In Germany, the trend of falling new infections could not be maintained. 2,200 new cases brought the total to 150,600.

Thursday, April 23, 2020

At home. New Zealand Day 29 Corona Alert Level 4.

New Zealand were at Alert Level 4 for five more days, while Germany had already had the first three days of the first wave of easing.

There was a novelty in today's New Zealand press conference. Five new infections were detected, but it was quickly discovered that these people, who returned to New Zealand from Uruguay, were already registered there. That is why the total number of reports was initially left to 1,451, because it was only with the WHO that it was intended to clarify whether a transfer of the reports from Uruguay to New Zealand should be made. Consequently, it was to prevent the WHO double counting from being included in their statistics. What a luxury problem, Sven thought. Later, the number was attributed to New Zealand. The previous day, 6,500 tests had been carried out. Because only a manageable number of contact persons had to be tested due to the small number of infected persons, a large part of the tests could be carried out in people who had no symptoms. So, it was already very good to carry out mass tests. These have now also been extended to pure Maori communities. The rules for opening up the retail trade have also been clarified. Unlike in Germany, shops are allowed to open regardless of their size, but customers are not allowed to enter the stores. Purchase and payment should be made online, the delivery must be absolutely contactless. The shops are free to organize the process in compliance with the hygiene and distance rules. Cash payments are only allowed in very specific exceptional cases. Mrs. Ardern made it very clear that the police would continue to detect and drastically punish violations.

In Germany, a Federal Parliament debate on the measures against Corona took place. Chancellor Merkel again failed to address the families of the victims. She very much regrets, she said, that individual federal states are too busy opening up. Of course, she didn't mention any by name. Sven's question remained as to what competences for imposing individual measures were in the federal government's position in the first place? World Medical Association President Montgomery told the press today that, in his view, a legal requirement to wear masks only makes sense for real protective masks, and considers scarves or scarves to be sufficient to be ridiculous. My speech, Sven commented. There has also been a public debate on the resources of health agencies with which they could make a full contact analysis. It was heard of the intention to create new jobs for this purpose. The actual number of employees was not known and certainly not known how comprehensive the contact analyses were already carried out. From the different statements, however, it was easy to see that the number of new infections was still far too high for this.

Sven: It has been reported in the media that 45% of the people in the major shopping streets of many big cities are already crowding compared to the weeks before the lockdown.

Friend-2: You have to see if this is a one-off effect or even more people are looking for the shopping experience like before the lockdown.

Sven: Yesterday I predicted that the solution approach of vaccination would be accompanied by a vaccination obligation. Today, Bavaria Prime Minister Söder was the first to speak out publicly in favor. I bet a box of wine that there will be a compulsory vaccination, not only in Germany.

Friend-3: I don't disagree.

Sven: I just found a message that men in particular will have to reach deeper into their pockets at the hairdresser in the future, as dry haircuts are no longer allowed for the time being. It is very astonishing how detailed the state suddenly intervenes in everyday life. Who was the adviser for this arrangement?

Friend-1: Blow-drying is also forbidden. Maybe therefore it will be a little cheaper.

Let's look at the current figures of the day for Germany. There was no significant decrease in new infections. Again, an increase from 2,500 to 153,100 was reported.

Friday, April 24, 2020

At home. New Zealand Day 30 Corona Alert Level 4.

The New Zealand society was quietly prepared for the concrete rules that would apply from the coming Tuesday with Alert Level 3. The number of daily tests had almost reached the 7,000 mark. A new record. The total was 108,000. It was noticeable that less than 1.4% of the people tested were positive. A world-high value. He explained that the field of mass tests had long since been advanced, while in most European countries, only close contacts and suspected cases were still being tested. Sven was also impressed by the fact that the Finance Minister continued to condole with the family of the man who died yesterday. The way he or Jacinda Ardern said these words sounded honest and compassionate. This was one of the reasons why the government had gained such a high reputation among the population.

In Germany, the debate on further easing dominated. The number of measures was too high to be able to keep an overview. Sven remembered a few examples:

In Berlin, the playgrounds are to be reopened from May 1.

In some provinces, concrete consideration is being given to the opening up of gastronomic facilities.

The first dates for the re-admission of divine services are mentioned. So far, the number of visitors was limited to ten.

The Bundesliga is coming into focus with the prospect that there will be football games again from mid-May. Spectators must not be in the stadium. Quarantine requirements must be observed. Half of the population was against the approval.

Other courts allowed demonstrations with up to 50 people.

The administrative court in the province Hessen, after a student's complaint, annulled compulsory schooling for the 4th grade in the primary school. With this, this federal state wanted to start teaching again soon. At first nothing came of it.

In opinion polls, support ratings for the CDU and Angela Merkel, Germans Chancellor, continued to rise.

The RKI also commented again. A spokesman said there could only be a promising contact tracing once the number of new infections had fallen to a few hundred a day. Germany was still a long way from that, despite the lockdown. Again, 1,900 new cases were added. In total, there were now 155,000. New Zealand had 1,461 infected people today, 5 more than the previous day.

Saturday, April 25, 2020

At home. New Zealand Day 31 Corona Alert Level 4.

In New Zealand, people celebrated "ANZAC Day". Every year on April 25, this national holiday is held in honor of all fallen soldiers and the surviving war veterans. It was a day of reflection, which is why no press conference was held. Of course, there was the daily press release with the latest figures. A further 5 new infected had been added. As a result, the number of new cases on each day of the last week was less than 10. The strategy seemed to work. 1,118 people were demonstrably healthy again. In total, New Zealand has so far claimed 18 Corona deaths.

In Germany, competition for further loosening ideas continued, albeit to a reduced extent, it was weekend. Now even the Health Minister himself questioned the 800 square meter rule. He also said he could imagine opening gyms in the near future. A permanent theme remained what concrete action had to be taken in order to be able to reopen the schools. There were no clear statements about kindergartens. Overall, however, the economic and financial aspects of the crisis now accounted for most of the columns of media reports.

Immense sums had already been invested in aid programs, a completely unmanageable size for the ordinary citizen.

In Germany, the number of infected cases rose by only 1,500 cases to 156,500. There have been fewer new infections reported on weekends in the past than during the week.

Sunday, April 26, 2020

At home. New Zealand Day 32 Corona Alert Level 4.

Even today was a quiet day in New Zealand. Once again, no press conference was held, but the statistical figures were published with the precision of a movement of a clock. In Germany, too, there was much calm on the political front. Only the President of the Federal Parliament stood out with a statement: Not everything had to resign from the protection of life, was the short version of one of his long intricate sentences. There was no debate on this.

People on the streets forgot more and more to keep the 1.5-meter distance. On their walk through the forest, Sven and Ling even met a group of ten people who clustered around a bench and held a picnic.

On this Sunday, the number of people infected in New Zealand increased by 5. At the same time, 6 people who had previously been considered as probably infected were shown to be always healthy. This number was therefore deducted again, so that the total number was now 1,469. As with every weekend, less was tested this time than during the week. The same was true of Germany. 1,300 new cases were found here, bringing the total to 157,800.

Monday, April 27, 2020

At home. New Zealand Day 33 Corona Alert Level 4.

Today was the last day New Zealand was at Alert Level 4. In the press conference, Dr. Ashley Bloomfield explained that from now on, cases with the status probably infected will no longer be reported to the WHO. Most other countries would only pass on the number of confirmed cases. New Zealand now wants to follow this unwritten rule and thus contribute to better comparability. He went on to say that Alert Level 3 would also maintain the obligation to quarantine or self-isolation for both confirmed and probable cases. The New Zealand Health Board however would also continue to count these cases in its statistics. Jacinda Ardern began her remarks with: "We are now eleven hours away from the transition to Level 3...". She again used the method of countdown, as Sven and Ling had already experienced on March 25. Then she gave an overview of what all New Zealanders have achieved together so far. Other important information included the fact that New Zealand now has a capacity of 8,000 tests per day. She described as extremely pleasing the fact that in the last few days well below 1% of those tested had a positive result. This is proof of the good progress made in the mass tests. Capacity and procedures at the health authorities were already sufficient to identify all contacts for 300 infected persons in a short period of time. Although the number of infected persons is consistently very low, these capacities will be significantly expanded in the coming days. She once again urged that the guidelines be strictly adhered to in the next phase. She also announced further decisions will be made on May 11. She herself will no longer hold the daily press conferences from tomorrow, Dr. Bloomfield will continue to do so. She thanked Dr. Bloomfield, who she had experienced as a great personality in the fight against COVID-19. It was a great honor for her, she continued, to work with him on the biggest challenge in New Zealand's history. Finally, she explicitly turned to the families of the 19 people who had previously died from the Corona virus. Her words were sincere and honestly compassionate.

On this Monday, 3 new infections were detected. The transition to Alert Level 3 therefore began with the following figures: 1,472 infected, of which 1,124 were confirmed and 348 were suspected cases. 1,214 people were reported as cured, with 19 deaths so far. 126,066 tests had been carried out.

In Germany, the mandatory mask-wearing came into force today. More and more flights arrived from China, fully loaded with protective equipment, because we were still far from providing surgical masks to all people. The discussion on additional easing continued. The Federal Government, whose warnings have often gone unheard in recent days, again made a change of strategy. It now supported regional differences in measures. It remained a general statement, concrete examples were not to be heard. The number of new infections fell again significantly. Only 1,000 new cases were added, and we now had a total of 158,800 infected cases.

Easing exercises

Tuesday, April 28, 2020

At home. New Zealand Day 1 Corona Alert Level 3.

New Zealand was back at Alert Level 3. Retail shops sold again, albeit only due to online or telephonic orders, the amount of allowed leisure activities had been expanded. Nurseries and primary schools resumed operations, but only for a small proportion of children. 400,000 workers were able to return to work. The central statement "Stay Home" continued to apply. Dr. Bloomfield gave today's press conference. He began by accurately listing the current data. He also explained how the cases of the recoveries are determined. Anyone who had no symptoms in the last 48 hours, whose positive test was ten days ago and who had received a corresponding medical diagnosis from a doctor, was considered to have recovered. In Germany, the number of recoveries was estimated by the RKI without informing the public of the underlying assumptions. In the second part of his speech, he reiterated the importance of strict compliance with Level 3 rules in order not to jeopardize the great success achieved in the last five weeks. He specified the goal: the erasure of the virus would not be achieved on a certain date with zero new infections, but only if there were no new cases over a period of months.

In Germany, the RKI caused astonishment. Today, the reproduction factor (R-factor), so dominantly raised to the fore in recent days, has only been described as one aspect of several as relevant to the achievement of the goals. Suddenly, the current number of new infections came into focus, as well as the need to fully understand them. The acute overload of health boards was cited as a problem. The number of daily new infections must drastically fall well below 1,000, otherwise it would be impossible to fully track the contacts without any gaps.

In one province, the Constitutional Court had ordered the lifting of the curfew. The Ministers of Education worked on a concept for the nationwide re-establishment of school operations. New Zealand reported only 2 new cases, 1,474 in total.

Wednesday, April 29, 2020

At home. New Zealand Day 2 Corona Alert Level 3.

Contrary to her announcement yesterday, Mrs. Ardern had reappeared at the press conference. There were probably many who did not want to miss her. With her own clear words, she went into the first day of Alert Level 3 and listed precisely which violations of the rules had already been reported and suspected. There were not only exhortations, but also arrests and criminal charges. She wanted to nip in the bud from the beginning any attempt to take everything a little looser. In Germany, new infections had settled for the third day in a row around the value just above 1000. Nothing worth to talk about. The economic outlook dominated the debate. Initial forecasts for the deep recession made the rounds. In New Zealand, the number of new infections was 2, 1,476 overalls. A total of 159,900 cases of infection have now been reported in Germany.

Thursday, April 30, 2020

At home. New Zealand Day 3 Corona Alert Level 3.

Mrs. Ardern reiterated her comments today on the nature and number of breaches of the conditions. She made it clear that the government is running a zero-tolerance line. She was relieved that the influx to the half-open primary schools was very low. Those who had the opportunity to continue learning at home should not go to school. Only 2% of primary school pupils returned to school. The proportion of children who went back to kindergarten was 4%.

Figures on unemployment and short-time working were published today in Germany. They were disastrous. In the afternoon, the Prime Ministers of the provinces met again with the chancellor. Some minor facilitations were agreed. Divine services would soon be possible again, museums and zoos should be able to open. Details are set at the country level, as always. A decision on more extensive measures will be taken on May 6.

Epilogue

Sven and Ling finished their daily recording today. Their everyday life was regulated by the pandemic specific regulations and laws in Germany. The prospect of an early return to the life known before March remained vague. The hope of returning to New Zealand in the next few weeks to continue their abruptly interrupted journey was unrealistic. New Zealand's borders would remain closed to foreigners, perhaps with the exception of Australia, for a long time to come. Nevertheless, they remained connected to New Zealand. In the first weeks of their holiday, they had not noticed the work of the government there. The fight against COVID-19 completely changed it. Since the lockdown, they have been constantly dealing with it. That will not change for the foreseeable future. Sven was initially unsure whether the New Zealand government had set itself the right goal in this crisis. But the administration had to make decisions. He was and remained impressed by how Mrs. Ardern and her entire cabinet filled this objective with clear measures and consistent, transparent communication piece by piece. Especially he was impressed how the "Team of 5-million" flighted the virus.

He had many days to read into the subject and meanwhile became a supporter of the not only New Zealand's approach: The Corona virus must be eliminated. He will be watching developments in New Zealand with interest and will be happy with the Kiwis if the goal of eradicating the virus is achieved.

It's me, the Virus

I'm Corona. I am also called COVID-19 or SARS-CoV-2. They say I'm "new." But I'm not that new, I'm one of many Corona viruses, albeit a special one. It's not up to me, but to people who deal with me, at least in part. There are really many of them. I myself am surprised by this extensive attention.

Numerous international teams of scientists have been researching with me and my Corona siblings for years. They've played through a lot of scenarios where I'm triggering a pandemic and panic. They didn't know when I was going to do it, but they were sure it would happen soon. Since I have been active, a lot of specialists from different fields of research have dealt with me. They give well-intentioned or interest-driven advice to politicians and governments who then make decisions. They always refer to me. They instrumentalize me. It was precisely these politicians who, with exceptions, have always accepted all these scenarios with negligent disinterest and indifference. At least they did nothing to prepare for me. There were not only the simulations of the scientists, there were real events in the last two decades, not only locally, which were triggered by my predecessor viruses. Have they taken any precautions on the basis of the experience of that time? If at all, then only a few. Most of them don't. Now that I am ubiquitous, they adorn themselves with their consultative virologists. At the same time, it seems to me that there is an industry that has always observed my development. It now appears quite vehemently, positioning itself with "recognized personalities" who want to take advantage of the hour. This pharmaceutical industry waited a long time for me. Now their great hour seems to have come.

I have succeeded in achieving what no other virus before me has achieved. I've changed the world, what do I say, I've taken it off the hook. I only needed three months to do so. I am an imposition on democracy, I heard from the mouth of the head of government of the country, in which politicians undeviating are maundering of "Maß und Mitte (German)". That means, don't lean towards any side, do not allow any fluctuation. Do they know that they borrowed this term from Confucius, the Chinese Philosopher? What a belittlement. I am also an imposition on dictatorships, autocracies, monarchies. I am an imposition on humanity. I'm global, I'm everywhere at the same time and already there if you're hesitant to run. I create fear. Well, it is not my intention to stoke fears, nor is it me that creates fear. It is the people who speak out about me to the people of their countries, indeed to the world population. Scientists, politicians, media. Their tone is the same in unison. It seems that it is I who has erased the eternal laws of thesis and antithesis. Opinions about me are the same everywhere. other opinions are suppressed. I searched the media, but I couldn't find the counter-thesis about me. Is there, for the first time in the history of humanity, an absolute truth that all the countries of the world have recognized almost simultaneously within just a few months? It didn't take global conferences to get an identical picture of me. The obvious conclusion is that I must be the evil, the devil in pure form.

I am not as cruel as you are told. If I manage to penetrate through your nose, mouth or eyes, I get stuck in a person's throat. Most of the time I am only with a few colleagues. Then we are weak. But we don't care, we just want to live somewhere, survive. Sometimes, however, a whole armada of us Coronas manages to make a successful journey to the lungs. I create fever and cough, occasional sniffles and fatigue or I turn off the sense of smell. But by and large I am passive and my wearers do not even know that I live in them. I myself know nothing about the effects of us Coronas all together, but I have been told that I am not or hardly felt by the vast majority of people I infect. I also infect people who are already sick and weak. People whose risk of dying is high, but who are still alive. Sometimes I'm the last drop on the hot stone. This is not my intention, but I have no influence on their whole organism. Then I kill without intent to kill. Those I kill, however, often know what led to their illnesses, which have weakened their bodies for a long time since I joined.

Thousands of statistics and metrics have been created about me from the first day of my appearance. Whenever I am proven in a human being, the counter is increased by "one" in the chart. And that not only once a day, but real time, as some call it. Well, there are also countries that leave it at daily updates. Isn't that crazy? Are there such statistics for other diseases that can be fatal, too? I haven't found them anywhere. Why are cancers not made public just as meticulously? Why are there no up-to-date statistics on flu, heart attack, diabetes? I would like to study them: On May 11, there were 77 diabetic diagnoses in country A, province B, district C. On May 12, 18 cases were added, making a total of 95. Today is May 13, again, 21 cases of proven diabetes have been reported, making it to 116. Why do you physicians and statisticians do this right now and exclusively with me? And that all over the world. Has everyone gone mad? Or is there an intention behind it? In order to fight me medically, you don't have to smash the world's population every hour with such a flood of data. Doctors can use them for their work, of course. So, do you do it to try out something bigger, to enforce it, maybe to establish it? If that is the intention, I will become a victim myself. Then I have become a cue ball for politicians and interest groups and, as a mostly harmless virus, I have to serve that those who have waited a long time for the favor of the hour want to use it now.

Tests were quickly developed to prove me. This makes sense because I accept that one wants to combat my bad influence on the health of some people. But why am I included in the statistics of the new cases even if one finds only minimal traces of me. This suggests to the consumer of the figures that the situation is very dangerous. At worst, 85% of all I'm demonstrable feel the symptoms of normal flu, and often they don't notice me at all. Well, at 15%, I am not so harmless. What exactly I do there is still a mystery for me. You research, you're on my heels. You discover something new every day. Some doctors believe that I can also suffer the heart, stomach, nerves, intestines and kidneys but this is still been investigated, so far this are assumptions. I have never, as far as I remember, killed a healthy person by my work alone. This is not only part of the truth, but must also be clearly shared with the public. If I have accelerated the death of a seriously lung suffering patient, then I will be cited as the cause of death in the statistics, not the lung disease that is the real cause. The same applies to heart disease or obesity. Death is always attributed to me. That is dishonest and not scientific at all.

When I first appeared in my current form, the people who treated the patients I infected knew nothing of me. That's normal. They cannot be accused of that. It takes a few cases to get closer to me, to understand me, the "novel" virus. As a result, I have also infected doctors and nurses. I am not responsible for the fact that there are countries in which I myself could still infect medical personal two months after I was proved and deciphered. Everything about me could be read early on in relevant publications. From the beginning there was an international exchange of information between scientists and political leaders were also informed. Some countries, especially in Asia, reacted quickly when they heard about me and had the first knowledge about my spread and impact. Too many countries, including many in the Western Hemisphere, waited. Why? For ideological reasons, have publications of certain scientists not been read, measures taken by certain countries have not been adopted? Or was recklessness, ignorance or even arrogance the real source for waiting? The fact that I can be anywhere in a global world within hours at the same time is a truism. This requires neither scientific nor political expertise. Anyone who wants to fight me successfully must not act in an ideologically driven manner. Whoever does so will deliberately make the people, for who's good they are responsible, suffer.

I don't know where and how I came into existence. Can anyone remember the minutes of his birth? Hardly. Later you learn about it from the parents and can read it in a document. I became known all over the world after Chinese virologists knew after initial uncertainty that I was a very special one among the Corona viruses. At the beginning of January, they had analyzed my gene structure and communicated it to the world public. In a very short time, tests were developed to track me down. But maybe I was already present in a human body in another part of the earth. Maybe they had seen me there as a cute flu virus. High-ranking scientists shouldn't be able to do that, but if I initially appeared only very sporadically, you can't immediately discover the complete novelty on me. Every knowledge takes time. There was never anyone who had the full certainty of it because of a one-off event. Especially recently I have been found in people who have died at about the same time as those in China but in other places of the world. I therefore advise you to continue to look objectively and consequently to find out where I really come from. Is it likely that there is exactly one place of my origin? Just as it is not certain that human life on Earth originated in exactly one place. Let me say it freely: My brothers, sisters, and I have gone to different areas of the earth and tried our luck. When one achieved it, we all were satisfied. Perhaps several of us have made it. This strategy of taking ownership is immemorial and should not surprise any expert. So, continue to search for my true origins. Perhaps you can learn something from this for the future. But don't make it a political game!

Yes, it is true, I kill occasionally. Mostly indirect, rarely direct. But other risk factors do the same as I do. Smoking frequently, excessive consumption of alcohol, obesity because of too much sugar, poor diet because of low quality food and more. There are dozens of illnesses or behaviors that cause death earlier than in a person who lives completely risk-free. In many cases, it has to do with the fact that the immune system does not work as it should. It is weakened by all the above factors. I don't weaken it any further, but I'll show you the consequences if your immune system is broken. Do you put the whole globe on the chain when smokers ruin their natural defense system, when car drivers who like to enjoy racing because of missing speed restrictions kill innocent people?

Why with me now? Is smoking banned worldwide? No! Is it forbidden to buy sickening food? No. Do you forbid, in a convivial round, to tip one liquor after another? No. Have you set a reasonable speed limit? Some countries have, Germany still does not consider it as necessary. Why are people now banned from convivially gathering? Just because I could infect some of them? Just because you loved the peculiar causes as a normal part of life? Or do you politicians not dare to take action against it, because otherwise supposed human friends will deprive you of their favor?

China had one goal from the beginning: to eradicate me. The leaders did not say it explicitly, and the people from the West, who are looking very distrustful at China anyway, have not recognized it. If they had registered it, they would have directed this goal into the realm of the fable. Not feasible! New Zealand have set themselves the same goal and communicated it clearly. That is why there it is extremely difficult for me to oppose it. If I don't get reinforcements, I'm going to lose the fight in New Zealand. In China, perhaps, too. But I don't care. There are so many other places in the world where I can continue to let off steam.

If the fight against me is to lead to a worldwide alliance, sooner or later I will have to give myself up. If I'm not too weak, I can retreat, hide, give my opponents a temporary triumph, and then come back next year in a slightly different form if I can regenerate. Or I'll die myself. That's normal. I, too, do not have the eternal right of existence.

I am very surprised that the strict measures that were first taken so consistently in the Middle Kingdom – often too late – have become the measure of all things all over the world. Keep distance, wash hands, wear masks, perform quick tests, go into quarantine, stop social gathering, even complete lockdown and much more. Well, all this can be medically justified. But the Western world, which always presents itself sublimely as a "free world" and thus, conversely, considers in particular China, as an "unfree world", also resorted to measures that were completely unthinkable only three months ago. Contact bans, the removal of freedom of movement, bans on work, invasion of privacy, the suspension of the right to education and much more, whatever has always been called inviolable human rights. The so-called "free world" and the so-called "totalitarian states" are now all doing the same thing. It was always unthinkable for me that I would ever have such a power. I am a tiny virus and within weeks I am changing the constitution of the whole globe. This is incredible. What is even more incredible, however, is that there are no critical voices on this. Or, if they are, they are not allowed to be heard. Where they are expressed, they are fought in the strongest possible terms.

As much as there is now this uniform action throughout the world, we must not forget that the need for it, which is always stressed today, has been recognized far too late. My genetic structure and mode of action in humans was known for a long time. It would have been so easy to do what the Chinese did immediately. But you had a tunnel view from the beginning. You stared at Hubei province and sought the atrocities and the death, staged the pictures and commented in a smart-alecky inflection. This was accompanied by the message that China is completely overextended with this challenge. Two mistakes resulted from this narrow-minded view: it was not noticed how China really acted in Hubei. It would have been easy to see that the package of measures had a chance of success. Secondly, it was not realized that I did not spread at all in almost all the other provinces of China, that I did not become a problem there because they prevented that there, I could infect a lot of people. The resolute actions of the Chinese have prevented me from spreading throughout the country. In any case, you did not want to learn from China. The consequences could be seen by mid-February at the latest, if you wanted to see them. Many still kept their eyes closed.

In addition, the people of China and the South-East Asian countries as a whole had taken up the fight against me, as well as New Zealand as from mid-March. What softened population structures did I encounter in the West? There, after four weeks of lockdown, people's suffering seemed so infinite that they pushed back to the old normality. Mind you, most of them suffered not from me, but from what the governments ordered for them.

It seems to be in the Western genes not to follow the Chinese project for fundamental reasons, but to postulate its own goals. This is legitimate, healthy competition, to eliminate me is a welcome approach. But that led to ideas as insane as infecting the whole country with me. Had anyone seriously thought about how me and my entire virus armada could develop, multiply, and change in millions of people? Does anyone have even the slightest idea of the consequences of a mass infection in three, five or ten years? Truly an insane plan. It was abandoned and now, in unison, only one possibility for my death is seen: vaccination. Whatever medium you use, whichever politician you listen to, the statements are always the same, word-like. "We have to live with the virus until there is a vaccine against it". The pharmaceutical industry is cheering. They adumbrate the business of the century, what do I say, the millennial business. Their lobbyists chat in almost casual tones about the fact that 7.5 billion people will be vaccinated, then the devil will be defeated, then I will be dead. Then human life is dead, I say. All experts know that developing a vaccine is a long process if the necessary tests are carried out meticulously. They also have a deep knowledge that there will be many side effects. Do they want to restrict people's lives in many ways up to this day and deprive them of basic rights? Do they have the intention of accepting the side effects that may cause physical harm or death to millions of people? Where is the alternative approach? Where is the contradiction to the vaccination gods?

I am only a virus and have a destiny that was given to me by creation. I cause illness and also kill when I encounter weak bodies. Targeted medical work combined with smart, truly global, i.e. ideology-free politics can defeat me if work is done to ensure a better immune system for all people. Promotes a healthy lifestyle, destroys disease-causing foods, and also takes care of the mental immunity system!

I call on you to rethink in the long term. If my existence makes sense, it is this. Of course, you should also fight me in the short term. Your measures to do this are largely alright. Nobody expects perfection in an acute situation. But if you are already putting your population on a leash, then the goal is to exterminate me. It can succeed, there are examples of this. But you will not be able to absolutely prevent death. If you are already trying to find out the number of "Corona Deaths" in your stats to justify your actions and celebrate your successes, please note that the number of deaths is not just a number in your damn tables. Notice that there are people behind the numbers who would live without me – maybe three more days, a month, half a year or even longer. Notice that these deceased have surviving members of their family who expect and deserve your words of compassion in order to cope with the loss a little better. Be honest and sincere. There are examples of state leaders you can follow.

Corona-Virus, May 2020

A Real Kiwi Bloke

Extract from the press release of the New Zealand Ministry of Health of 2 May 2020:

»Sadly, today we are reporting the death of a resident of Rosewood Rest Home who was transferred to Burwood Hospital. George Hollings was in his 80s, and his family have asked us to share his name and some information about him. George had a lot of friends who the family don't have contact details for and they'd like for them to have the opportunity to grieve along with his family. His family tell us that George will be remembered as a real Kiwi bloke, a rough diamond, who loved his deer stalking. They ask for the media to respect their privacy and to give them time to grieve. His family also say the staff who cared for George did an exemplary job. „We can't speak highly enough of the care Dad received. You've clearly chosen the best, most compassionate staff to work at Burwood.

George was considered to be a probable case of COVID-19, and he also had underlying health conditions. He passed away early this morning.

Every person we lose to COVID-19 is a tragedy, with a family and friends left without their loved one. Our thoughts are with George's family today and in the coming days. There have now been 20 deaths from COVID-19 in New Zealand.«

Manfred Görk

Luluba

Geschichte einer chinesischen Bauernfamilie

German Edition

Novel

408 pages – Paperback

In February 2018, Chen Yangwa died at the age of 88. He lived as a farmer in Luluba, a village in China's Shaanxi Province. Mengnan, one of his six daughters, wants to remember him as a special person. In the hour of death, her father's soul manages to save all his memories. In this way, in dialogue with Mengnan, she can poignantly trace the development of his large family. A life between tradition, rise and modernity, hunger, diligence and prosperity, tension and harmony. Chen Yangwa's only son and his two eldest daughters remain in the village and live as farmers in their ancestral roles. His other four daughters seize the opportunities in fast-developing China and leave their homeland without ever losing their close ties to the family. The author of this family saga lets the reader immerse himself deeply in a China that only a few know. The novel is given its peculiarity by the fact that everything it describes about the life of the family actually happened in this way. This makes it authentic, honest and fascinating.

BoD – Books on Demand, Norderstedt, Germany

Manfred Görk

Land der Mitte

Impressionen aus einer anderen Welt

German Edition

Travel Guide

2000 pages – Paperback

The well-travelled author conveys in a knowledgeable and entertaining way what special features you can expect on a trip to China, but without getting lost in the striking list of sights, hotels or restaurants of conventional travel guides – a travel guide of a very special kind! He also wants to make people curious about China by offering numerous seemingly random but representatively selected narratives of the everyday experience. All reports are authentic and provide an exciting insight into Chinese culture. Through this combination, the book is a great enrichment for all those who are interested in China and it makes you want to experience the fascinating empire of the middle.

Novum Verlag, Germany